Baking Up a Murder

Baking Up a Murder

A MYSTERY

Hattie Fox

NEW YORK

Published in the United States by Crooked Lane Books, an imprint of
The Quick Brown Fox & Company LLC.

Library of Congress Catalog-in-Publication data available upon request.

ISBN (hardcover): 979-8-89242-601-5
ISBN (paperback): 979-8-89242-602-2
ISBN (ebook): 979-8-89242-603-9

Cover design by Lulu Dubreuil

Printed in the United States.

www.crookedlanebooks.com

Crooked Lane Books
34 West 27th St., 10th Floor
New York, NY 10001

First Edition: March 2026

The authorized representative in the EU for product safety and compliance is eucomply OÜPärnu mnt 139b-14, 11317 Tallinn, Estonia,
hello@eucompliancepartner.com, +33757690241

10 9 8 7 6 5 4 3 2 1

For my niece, Marinna
Words will never be enough to
express how deeply I miss you.
Your light, your imagination, and your
beautiful spirit will remain
with me always.
I know you would have been an
extraordinary author, and I will carry
your story in everything I write.

Chapter One

The week of the funeral, we kept the bakery closed.

The entire time Grandpa Victor spent in the hospital and then hospice, the bakery had stayed open every day. I'd been here for months, keeping the bakery running while my grandma, my parents, and a rotating cast of aunts and uncles kept my grandpa company during the day. I stayed at my grandparents' empty house and slipped out early every morning, long before the sun rose, just as we used to do together when I was a child visiting and watching my grandpa bake. I followed his recipes and kept the bakery well-supplied with Danish kringles and other local specialties, as much as it pained me to leave behind the recipes I was truly passionate about: flaky croissants, delicate pastries, napoleons, and éclairs. I'd go to Grandpa's bedside after a long day at the bakery, flour-dusted and tired, and he'd beam at me, knowing I was doing just what he'd asked—keeping his work alive.

All that time, open despite everything, and now the bakery was dark. A *closed* sign hanging on the door in the middle of the day. I was sitting on the counter, the box of Grandpa Victor's recipe cards in my lap. At this point, I had them memorized, but you couldn't pay me to get rid of these cards, handwritten with smudged ballpoint pen in my grandfather's careful all-caps.

The door jingled and I almost dropped the box, turning to face the customer and tell them that we weren't open—and maybe we'd never be open again. When I went back to Los Angeles, the bakery would have to close its doors forever. My grandma in a kitchen was like a bull in a china shop. If the china shop was flammable and the bull had a knack for sparking flames and a propensity to mix up salt and sugar.

Instead of a customer at the door, it was Grandma Ruth, standing just inside the door, her hands on her hips as she gazed at the shadowy bakery.

"What are you doing sitting in the dark?" she asked, reaching for the light switch. The bakery flickered into its usual brightness, illuminating the dark circles under Grandma Ruth's eyes.

"Did you sleep at all?" I asked, sliding the recipe box off my lap.

Grandma Ruth shrugged slightly, smiling ruefully.

"I thought I'd come in and clean up a little," I said. "I left it in a bit of a state."

I'd been here on Tuesday, prepping and baking in the wee hours of the morning, when the call had come in that Victor had passed in his sleep. I'd turned off the ovens and crammed everything haphazardly into containers to deter bugs, but there was flour on the counters and nothing was in its place.

Before I could say anything else, Grandma Ruth let herself behind the counter and pulled the broom off its hanger on the wall.

I opened my mouth to protest, but she was already wagging a finger. "I need something to do," she said.

I slid off the counter and followed her around the bakery, packing away ingredients properly and throwing out week-old cookies that had never made it off their baking sheet. Between the two of us, cleaning took hardly any time at all, and before long, I was elbow-deep in suds, washing the last of the mixing bowls I'd left in the sink the day the call came.

"Madeline," Grandma Ruth said, leaning against the counter beside me as I washed. "You've been a real godsend to your grandpa and me these past few weeks. I don't know what I would've done without you—gone crazy, I guess."

"Stop, Ruth. I've only done what any family member would do."

"I don't see any other granddaughters or grandsons around here baking their butts off," Grandma Ruth said, craning her neck to look back toward the front of the bakery and back toward the pantry for dramatic effect. "This has been all you, kiddo, and I'm sorry I've been so busy taking care of Victor to not express how grateful I am until now."

"I miss him," I said. Sometimes the simplest but truest words were the best comfort. "I know he's only been gone a few days, but it feels like things will never be quite as bright without him."

"I know just what you mean. Honestly, I'm grateful I'll be kept busy closing up shop the next few weeks. It will be good to have the distraction." She tapped her chin. "Eventually, I'll have to get a job somewhere else, keep saving up for retirement . . . selling this place will go a little ways, but the real estate market's not too hot. Anyway, it'll be good to keep busy. It's not in my nature to just sit around and do nothing, is it?"

The soapy water suddenly felt ice-cold. I'd always planned to return to my life in LA and the delightfully posh French restaurant where I worked as the pâtissier. My cozy, yet tiny, apartment with the plants in the window that were always on the verge of death. The rather charming French sommelier at the restaurant, James, who I'd barely gone on one date with before my mom called to tell me that Victor had been hospitalized.

When I left LA, my job, my life there, it was supposed to be just for a week or two, to keep the business going until Victor got out of the hospital and back into the kitchen. Then my grandfather got worse, and it became a way to keep up the bakery's income for Victor and Grandma Ruth as the medical bills piled up.

Now, I wasn't sure. My half-glamorous, half-gritty life in the kitchen of Le Tableau Bleu felt so far away now, and none of it felt important anymore. What did it matter if I made the best, most gourmet éclairs in the Southern California food scene? What did a review in a food magazine mean if I was miles away from all my family as they grew older?

I withdrew my pruney hands from the water and dried them on the nearest dish towel, a novelty one embroidered with one of the windmills that were a signature of this gloriously Danish-themed town.

"Well," I started, but my phone buzzed in my pocket. Grandma Ruth waved for me to answer, and I took it into the café area.

"Hello?"

"Madeline," a stern, unyielding voice rang out, and I knew immediately it was Randall, my boss back at the restaurant. Speak of the devil.

"Yes," I said. "Hi."

"Did you get my email Thursday?" Randall asked. I heard clanging in the background and checked my watch they were just getting ready to open.

I cringed. "Yes," I said. "Sorry, I forgot to reply." He'd asked for an update on my leave of absence—and griped that my interim replacement's chocolate fillings were always grainy. It was his way of paying a compliment.

"So?" he said. "When can we expect you back?"

I peered past the counter to where Grandma Ruth was finishing rinsing off the mixing bowl I'd abandoned. She was humming under her breath, and once she hoisted the massive metal bowl onto the drying rack, I watched as her shoulders slumped and she let out a long sigh.

She and I had been avoiding the conversation about what would happen to the bakery once Victor passed. During the entire time I'd been staying here, running the bakery, today was the first time either of us had broached the subject. I knew Grandma Ruth couldn't learn to bake: I'd had the misfortune of eating a box-mix pancake she cooked once. She was good with the business side, but Victor had always been the baker. My parents and Grandma Ruth and Victor's other kids couldn't take it over—they weren't bakers, and they had their own jobs and lives elsewhere anyway. Without me, the bakery was done. I couldn't even imagine Grandma Ruth getting a job somewhere else—some soul-sucking, lonely position at a big company? An exhausting minimum-wage job at a restaurant or café? And she'd be alone, her coterie of gal pals aside.

"Actually," I said, turning back to the front of the store, with the adorable arched windows and the sights of Solvang, California, beyond them. The midday crowd was bustling by, locals on their way back from their lunch breaks and tourists on their way to the windmills. The hills in the distance that I knew sheltered the vineyards that had boomed in recent years here.

I cleared my throat. "I'm going to resign."

There was a clatter from the kitchen, and as I listened to my now ex-boss hem and haw and curse about how he'd have to find someone better than the current temp to take my place, I held up a hand to keep Grandma Ruth at bay. She stood feet away from me, her hands raised at her sides in disbelief.

When I hung up, I could only shrug at her. "I want to stay," I said, and she silently folded me into her arms. When she let go, she kept her hands on my shoulders.

"But what about LA?" she said. "Won't you miss it?"

"I'd miss you more," I teased. She looked at me sternly, and I sighed. "I *will* miss baking French pastries. But my only real friend there just moved to New York, and my rent's supposed to go up in a few months. The restaurant is exciting, but I never really cared about that. I just want to bake."

Grandma Ruth turned away and looked at the bakery cases, perfectly empty and waiting for the next batch.

"If you're staying," she said, "I want you to make it yours. Victor would want that too."

"Well, I could find a few more Danish recipes . . ."

"No," Grandma Ruth said. She rifled through the cards in the recipe box. "Do your own recipes. Make it French."

I forced a chuckle. "Ruth, this is a Danish-themed town."

Solvang was like something straight out of a fairy tale—a tiny European village made up of cute cottages with white walls and shingled roofs, with its very own windmills and cobblestone streets. The fact that the town was nestled in Southern California, three hours outside of Los Angeles, only added to its magical quality. It was like a storybook mirage amid the rolling hills of the Santa Ynez Valley.

Like the other bakeries in town, Victor and Grandma Ruth's bakery had always specialized in Danish desserts, a natural fit for Grandpa Victor, whose father had immigrated from Denmark. Grandpa Victor's signature item was a spandauer, a round pastry with a jam center and glazed with white icing. It was Grandpa Victor's secret recipe and their most popular dessert. French pastries would be heresy in these parts.

"That's my condition," Grandma Ruth said as she clutched Grandpa Victor's recipe cards to her chest. "If you're going to quit your job and move here, I'm not letting you be the pastry chef unless you make *your* recipes."

I couldn't help but smile.

"Okay," I said. "Deal."

Chapter Two

Two months later

"Do you have any apple skiers?"

The customer leaned over the bakery counter. She wore a red bonnet tied below her chin. Two long blonde braids were attached to the bonnet and hung well below her own natural, shortly cropped hair. Her husband, perusing the far end of the bakery counter, wore a plastic Viking helmet.

"I think you mean *æbleskiver,*" I said gently.

"Yes, that's it! I've heard they're the thing to get here. What are they exactly?"

"Sort of like a pancake ball," I explained patiently, and certainly not for the first time. "You must be visiting us from out of town."

"How'd you know?" the woman asked, tugging on the end of one of her artificial braids.

Between their novelty headgear, comfortable footwear and the series of shopping bags they each clutched, she and her husband both practically screamed "tourist." But I knew this routine well enough by now and played my part adroitly.

"Oh, just a lucky guess. I'm afraid we don't sell æbleskiver here. It's a Danish pastry."

"What *isn't* Dutch around here?" asked the husband, stepping over to join his wife.

"Danish," I corrected. "But this is a French pâtisserie. I'm Madeline Andersen, the owner. We don't have any æbleskiver or kringles. But we do have a lot of other things—croissants, petit fours. And our specialty of the house—éclairs. Here, give one of the pistachio crèmes a try. I made them myself this morning."

I cut one of the fresh éclairs neatly in half and handed the two pieces over to the tourist couple. The woman looked a bit suspiciously at the light green pistachio cream, but they both dutifully devoured their portion of éclair within seconds.

"Wow," said the husband. "That's great! And I don't even like pistachios!"

"Do they come in other flavors?" asked the wife.

"They sure do," Grandma Ruth said, walking over from the register where she'd just finishing ringing up a customer. "Let me show you . . ."

I let Grandma Ruth take it from there, satisfied that my latest batch of éclairs had won us another couple of converts. Now if only the locals were as easy to convince as the tourists, we'd be doing big business. But building a local customer base had proven an uphill battle ever since the bakery's grand reopening. Owning my own bakery had been a lifelong dream of mine, though the reality was proving to be more of a mixed bag. Certainly I had never envisioned that my dream French bakery would be located in a Danish tourist town.

I grew up visiting my grandma and grandpa in Solvang throughout my childhood and teens. Every summer my parents took a two-week cruise with their closest friends, the

Martindales. Most kids would have been upset at being left behind, but I looked forward to their annual departure because it meant I got to visit Grandma Ruth and Victor.

The picturesque town was truly magical to me as a child, and there was always something to do. Solvang thrived on the tourist trade, whether it was folks stopping over for a few hours while on their way to LA or Angelenos seeking a break from the city. Even outside of its quaint architecture, walkable downtown and many small independent shops and businesses, Solvang had a surprising amount to offer. There were a series of annual festivals, such as Danish Days and Julefest, the Christmas celebration, and now the vineyards offered additional upscale activities for adults.

But even more than the town itself, I'd always looked forward to spending time here, in the bakery. It was already several decades old when I would visit as a kid, well-established in the community with a thriving customer base of locals and tourists. I was enthralled by everything in the bakery back then—the industrial-sized mixers I could literally sit in as a child; the constant, comforting scent of cinnamon and sugar; and, of course, the endless rows of desserts. I loved waking up while it was still dark outside to go with my grandma and grandpa to the bakery and begin the morning baking, watching with pride as they joked and chatted with the stream of customers who came in throughout the day.

Those summer visits were pure magic and were the reason I first dreamed of becoming a baker. Unlike most of my high school peers I knew exactly what career I wanted to pursue and went straight to culinary school after graduation. A post-grad six-month sojourn in Europe, eating my way through some of the most famed bakeries and restaurants in the world, convinced me that French baking could not be beat. I became obsessed with all things patisserie and upon returning to LA got my first job as an assistant pastry chef at a posh French restaurant. The LA restaurant scene was fierce and competitive—and I loved every minute of it. I worked my way slowly but steadily up the ranks throughout my early twenties, moving up to better and better restaurants until I was finally named head pastry chef at Le Tableau Bleu, an up-and-coming French fusion spot beloved by young Hollywood.

It only made sense that I would return to the place that inspired me to bake in the first place.

I shook myself from my reverie as Grandma Ruth finished ringing up the tourist couple's purchase—a box of éclairs for themselves plus several boxes of macarons to take to friends and family members back home. I watched with pride as she chatted them up, just like the old days when she and Grandpa Victor ran the bakery. I hoped to foster the same community feel that always seemed to come so naturally to them. Though not everything was the same: I'd certainly instituted some major cosmetic changes to the place, along with completely changing the entire menu.

We used some of Grandpa Victor's life insurance money to totally renovate the space. We traded the traditional but old and gouged dark wood and red Danish flags for durable marble countertops and lots of vintage mirrors on the wall, with brass accents like you'd find in many a Parisian patisserie. There were small white iron tables and matching chairs placed in front of the shop and a charming vintage chandelier I found at the local flea market hung from the ceiling. The lighter, airer décor made the small space seem twice as large and allowed greater focus on the baked goods in the long, wraparound bakery counter. The pastel petit fours, flower-draped cakes, and éclairs frosted in a variety of colors practically dazzled. It perfectly matched the dream I'd long held in my head for my own bakery—even if we were embedded in a Danish-themed town.

But I'd figured that specializing in French baked goods would give us a competitive edge, once the locals could get over the shock. There were already several other bakeries in the small town that churned out all of the traditional Danish treats that visitors came seeking. We offered a literal different flavor. The one Danish recipe I'd insisted on keeping was Grandpa Victor's signature spandauers, which we still made using his handwritten recipe. The French motif seemed to be working with the tourist crowd. They might initially stumble in expecting the usual fare, but they left happy after tasting our wares. The locals, however, were proving to be a different matter entirely. Locals like Marcus, who walked in just as the tourist couple headed out.

"Good morning, Mrs. Nielsen," Marcus boomed. He seemed capable of only speaking at a high volume. It might have been due to his job as one of the drivers of the horse-drawn carriages that carted tourists up and down Main Street. He had to speak loudly to be heard in the open-air carriages above the traffic noise as he enlightened guests on Solvang's history and local spots of interest.

"G'morning, Marcus!" Grandma Ruth boomed back at him. "How's business?"

"The usual. Up and down the street. The summer crowd is here so we're keeping busy. Can I get a black coffee and a spandauer?"

"You surely can. And how about one of our napoleons as well?"

Marcus scrutinized the contents of the bakery counter for a minute before saying, "Naw, I'm good."

"Marcus Belamy!" Grandma Ruth said sternly. "You've been coming in here every morning for weeks and only buy black coffee and a spandauer. And I know you could eat more than that—you're not missing any meals," she said, shooting a meaningful glance at Marcus's ample tummy.

"Ruth!" I hissed, feeling my face flush.

Grandma Ruth barreled on, undeterred. For decades she'd served as assistant coach for the high school football team. The *boys'* high school football team. It was an unusual gig for a woman in this town, but she genuinely loved the sport, and they'd needed the help. Marcus was just one of the many former players she'd coached, and she easily slipped back into coach mode with them. "Back in the day you never left without one or two—or three—cookies in hand. And now it's just 'black coffee, black coffee.' What's wrong with all this?" she said, giving a wide sweep of her arm that encompassed the length of the bakery counter.

"Shoot, Coach. This is all just a bit . . . delicate. I don't go for really fancy foods. Just give me a plain cake doughnut or a spandauer and I'm happy. You've always had the best ones in town."

"Well, maybe if you actually tried something new, you'd find that you liked it," Grandma Ruth continued. "Here, I'm charging you for this napoleon."

I stood by, too mortified to intervene as Grandma Ruth boxed up a napoleon along with Marcus's usual to-go cup of black coffee. I waited until he'd slunk sheepishly out the door to say my piece.

"Grandma! You can't bully the customers into buying things! At least give them a free sample. And you also can't fat shame them!"

"Firstly, I don't even know what 'fat shaming' is. Secondly, we're never going to get this place humming again if we don't take a stronger approach with the locals. You know I believe in your talent, Madeline."

"I know."

"But people around here have a small-town attitude. They're resistant to change. They like the same old things. We have to find ways to get them to take notice."

I knew she was right, but I was at a loss as to how to win over the local crowd. I'd always let my baking speak for itself. Had my years working at posh restaurants in LA made me disconnected from regular folks' taste? Where I saw sleek simplicity in the bakery's new look, did they see only pretension? Not for the first time I found myself worrying about my now entwined financial future with Grandma Ruth. If the patisserie went under, it wouldn't just be my failure. I'd be dragging her down with me, and she was the last person on earth I'd want to hurt.

As if sensing my worried thoughts, Pepper, my cat, pressed herself against my leg. I was about to reach down to give Pepper a scratch for providing some much-needed comfort when Grandma Ruth called out.

"Uh-oh. Here come the cops."

Chapter Three

"What do you mean the police are here?" I asked Grandma Ruth, a slight note of panic in my voice.

But before she could answer, the vintage brass bell above the bakery door chimed as a man strode inside.

Grandma Ruth was known for her hyperbole (or "being colorful" as she preferred to term it). So rather than several armed police officers invading the bakery, sirens blaring, in walked a solitary man in a pair of tight-fitting jeans and a snug navy polo. A rather handsome man, with a swath of dark stubble, thick eyebrows, and a piercing stare now directed fully at me. He strode confidently up to the bakery counter, never breaking eye contact.

"How can I help you, uh . . . Officer?" I asked nervously.

"I see Ruth has tipped you off," he said glancing over at my grandma, who just shrugged and gave a half smile in our direction. "You can just call me Ash. Technically it's Detective Ashton, but everyone calls me Ash."

"I'm Madeline. Madeline Andersen."

"Isn't a madeline a type of cookie?"

"That's a madeleine, not a Made*line*," I said. "But it is a bit ironic, right? So tell me, are you here on . . . official business?"

"Only semi-official," he said with a wry smile. He seemed a bit bemused by my nervousness. "I wanted to introduce myself and sample some of your goods. Er, baked goods, that is. I've heard they're delicious."

Grandma Ruth chimed in. "You'll have to pay. This isn't some sort of police shakedown for free food."

"*Grandma*!" I admonished, feeling a flush of embarrassment for the second time that morning.

But the detective just laughed. "Of course I'll pay. I believe in supporting local businesses." He turned back toward me and said, "Ruth was my football coach back in high school. So I'm used to her taking a stern hand with me. Back then I especially needed it."

"He was a wild one," Grandma Ruth confirmed as the bell above the door announced the arrival of another customer. I made a note to ask her later how on earth she was once a *football* coach and I'd never heard about it until recently.

The woman who entered was sharply dressed and had sleek black hair down to her shoulders. Based on her business casual attire I pegged her as a resident rather than a tourist. Between her and Ash's arrival I figured my luck with the locals just might be turning around. As Grandma Ruth busied herself assembling some sweets for Ash, I went over to greet the new arrival.

"Bonjour! Can I help you with anything?"

"I'm just here to look around," the woman said curtly. "Do you use French butter in all your baking?"

I was a bit taken aback by her abrupt question but answered, "Why, yes. Yes, of course. I try to only use the most authentic ingredients in everything."

The woman bent down and peered with great intensity into the bakery case. She tapped the glass, as if tapping the side of an aquarium. Suddenly, she let out a shriek.

I jumped, startled at her screech. "What? What's wrong?" I asked frantically.

"Is that a cat?" the woman yelped, pointing dramatically over at Pepper, who was curled up in his cat bed behind the counter.

Unimpressed with the woman's outburst, Pepper only briefly opened his eyes before resuming his nap.

"Oh," I said, relieved. "Yes! That's just my cat, Pepper. He's sort of the bakery's mascot."

"A cat? In a bakery? That's unhygienic! Someone should report you to the police!" the woman said loudly.

Ash strolled over to us. His ears must have perked up at the word "police."

"Is everything okay over here?" he asked with the same bemused twinkle in his eye from before.

"Who wants to know?" the customer demanded, seemingly unimpressed by Ash's good looks and friendly demeanor. I couldn't relate.

"I'm Detective Ashton," he explained. "With the Solvang Police Department."

"Oh, good. I want to file a report. This place is in violation of the health code."

"No, we're not," I said, slightly indignantly. Having worked in the LA restaurant scene for several years, I'd certainly dealt with my fair share of fussy patrons, and often outright rude ones. But this woman seemed positively unhinged.

"Pepper is allowed to be here," Grandma Ruth said indignantly, hustling over to us. "We have the paperwork to prove it!"

It was true. Grandma Ruth was good friends with the health inspector. They'd grown close over the course of his annual inspections of the bakery. When he was undertaking the preliminary before our grand reopening, I'd casually mentioned I had a pet cat that I worried was lonely while locked up in the house all day. The inspector explained that you could apply for special zoning to allow animals on the premises, which I promptly did.

"Okay, *grandma*," the woman sneered, and I raised a hand to stop her. *Nobody* called Ruth *grandma* but me—and even then, only when I was a little mad at her. She told all of us grandkids from the moment we could speak that we'd better learn how to pronounce "Ruth." Once I was a teenager and got into her good graces, I'd found that I could get away with the occasional "Grandma" when she knew she was being devious and that I was teasing her back.

"Please," I said and lowered my hand. "I can show you the certificate, if you like, but I assure you he's allowed to be here, and that we take the necessary precautions when we're preparing food to keep workspaces clean. But this is a pet-friendly space, if you saw the sign on the door."

Since I started bringing Pepper to work, I'd realized we might be able to make some extra dough—literally and figuratively—by also baking and selling pet treats. Now I had a small section of the bakery counter devoted to dog and cat treats made from a variety of simple ingredients like pumpkin and grains, and several regulars who came in on all fours.

"He's really docile," I said, plucking a small "cat cookie" from the case and dropping it in front of Pepper. He awoke just long enough to devour the treat before settling back to sleep.

"It's disgusting," the woman said. "I don't want a dusting of cat hair on my éclairs. I'm certainly never buying anything from here." And then she stalked out the door, the bell chiming after her.

I could only let out a tired sigh as she disappeared down the street.

"Good riddance," murmured Grandma Ruth. "What a nutjob."

"I'm sorry about all that," I said sheepishly to Ash.

"Don't worry about it," he said. "I happen to love cats. But I'd better get back to work." He grabbed the white box tied with string that Grandma Ruth had assembled for him. "Oh, and I almost forgot—Lars down at City Hall asked me to drop these flyers off around town. Would you mind putting some out?"

"No problem," I answered, accepting the stack of papers without looking at them and placing them on the counter behind me.

"I'll see you around, I'm sure," Ash said as he loped toward the door. "It's a small town, after all."

I remained in the same spot for a few extra seconds after Ash had departed, lost in very different thoughts about our two recent visitors. Behind me, Grandma Ruth was scanning one of the flyers that Ash had dropped off.

"Madeline," she exclaimed. "Our prayers have been answered!"

She thrust the flyer into my hands. "There's going to be a baking competition in town. It's coming up in a few days, but you still have time to enter."

I quickly read the flyer and made a face. "But it's probably a contest for amateur bakers, right? That leaves me out."

"Anyone can enter. There's nothing in the rules that says you can't—see the bottom of the page? Besides, I heard Sylvia from that bakery over by the new vineyard that she was entering some kind of competition—it must be this! So I think you should enter too," Grandma Ruth said, her eyes sparkling with enthusiasm.

I looked at her doubtfully. "I don't know, Ruth. I've never really been much for competitions."

"Ah, but that's the beauty of it," Grandma Ruth said. "To pulverize everyone and get the prize." I could see her competitive side coming out. She must have been an intense football coach—I'd seen enough of how she yelled at games on TV when the Raiders were playing.

"*Is* that the beauty of it? I'm pretty sure the competition is about creativity and originality, not pulverizing people," I laughed.

"Okay, but you have a great sense of creativity, Madeline. You could come up with something truly unique and amazing."

"But everyone will expect Danish pastries. It wouldn't feel right using one of Grandpa Victor's recipes when all of my specialties are French."

"That's exactly why this is the perfect opportunity! You can win with one of *your* recipes and prove to the town how good they are!"

I looked at her, still hesitant. "I don't know if I have time to prepare. I'm pretty busy with work here."

"You can make time," Grandma Ruth said firmly. "This could be a great opportunity for you. You're sure to win."

I considered Grandma Ruth's words. I'd always admired her drive and passion for the things she loved. No doubt she was trying to get me to have that same je ne sais quoi. And the idea of potentially winning the prize and getting my name out there *was* tempting.

"Okay," I said finally. "I'll think about it."

Something told me that Grandma Ruth would get her way and I would be entering the contest. I couldn't help but feel a little excited about the idea. Maybe, just maybe, I could surprise myself and show off my baking skills to everyone. Maybe I'd reach people who hadn't yet come into the shop and get new customers out of it.

Grandma Ruth smiled triumphantly. "That's all I ask. And if you need any help, you know I'll be right there beside you. I've still got a few tricks left in these old hands."

She gave my arm a reassuring pat before heading toward the kitchen, whistling like she already knew I'd won. I stood there a moment longer, imagining the contest full of people tasting my pastries, and my shop's name whispered between their bites. Maybe this wasn't just about Grandma Ruth getting her way. Maybe this was the start of something bigger.

Chapter Four

"What is she up to now?" Grandma Ruth gestured with a spatula at the dark-haired customer at the bakery counter.

"She appears to be examining the éclairs for cat hair again," I said with a sigh.

"I think she's trouble," Grandma Ruth said.

I couldn't say that I disagreed with my grandmother. We were both surprised when the woman had returned after briefly trying to have us shut down for a supposed health code violation. But since that incident she'd shown up several times. She never bought anything, just looked around briefly before departing. Pepper wisely made himself scarce when she showed up, perhaps remembering her diatribe. And here she was again and did indeed seem to be up to no good. And not just because she was taking notes while looking at the éclairs in the front display case.

The bakery was bustling with patrons today. The aroma of freshly brewed espresso and warm croissants filled the room, but it didn't distract me from the woman's piercing gaze. There was no escape as she approached the register, her eyes drilling into me like a dagger. She had caused enough drama already, and now she clearly wanted something from me. I had no choice but to obey. I pulled at my pink apron nervously and stepped up to the counter, already dreading the conversation about to come.

Her behavior today had caught not only my attention but that of the other customers too. Her eyes were wide, and she kept glancing around nervously, as if worried someone might approach her, and her pale cheeks were flushing pink more and more with every passing moment. Every now and then, she would mutter to herself and fidget with her fingers, causing those nearby to exchange puzzled glances.

Though the way she acted was strange enough, most of my uneasiness about her came from the fact that she seemed unhappy with what she saw—but never tasted—at my bakery. During each of her brief visits she had taken notes. At first, I thought she might be compiling notes for the health board, but that didn't seem to be the case. I was beginning to take her actions personally. I had no idea what she had against me, but it was definitely something. Was she ever going to let me know what her problem was? Had she previously bought something from the bakery that she didn't like? If so, I would have gladly given her a refund if she would have just communicated her displeasure with my baked goods. If there was another reason . . . what was it? We were both new to Solvang, so how could she already have a beef with me?

"I heard she just moved here from Georgia," Grandma Ruth whispered as she stuffed a lock of her silver hair back into her hair net. "New to town, and already picking fights? I find that suspicious."

Grandma Ruth hadn't needed to make that announcement for me to know that she didn't find the woman trustworthy. Grandma Ruth's raised eyebrow and glare were good indications that she didn't trust this non-customer farther than she could throw her. I'd only seen her like this once before, and that was with an old neighbor kid who picked on me one summer I was staying with Grandma Ruth and Victor.

"What's her name again?" I whispered back.

"My name is Mallory," the woman announced loudly. "And yes, I did move here from Atlanta. Why do you feel the need to talk about me?"

I thought I'd been quiet with my whisper. Realizing otherwise, I cringed. I'd have to smooth over the situation.

"It's just that we like to meet anyone new in town," I said weakly. "And you're . . . new in town."

Should I offer her a free pastry to make up for what we'd said? No doubt, based on her earlier complaints, she wouldn't want one anyway. But why was she back if she hated the baked goods here so much?

Never mind her reasons; I didn't want to come off as rude. I also didn't want to have a reputation for gossiping about customers. What I *did* want to be known for were my delicious pastries. I put a lot of time and effort into making sure that they came out perfectly. It was a passion for me. It was the whole reason why I had agreed to take the bakery over in the first place; the shop was a way for me to share my love of baking and to help my grandma stay afloat.

One of our few regulars, a middle-aged man with a thick Southern accent, approached the counter. Mr. Flannery came in every morning and was sweeter than the sweetest macaron I'd ever created.

"Madeline, is everything all right?" he asked in a concerned tone.

Mallory looked over at him with a scowl. "Why wouldn't it be all right? Are you asking that because of *me*?"

"No, no, I didn't say that," he said, trying to calm her down. "I just heard raised voices."

The only raised voice had been Mallory's, but I suppose that was neither here nor there.

"I simply wanted to tell her that the éclairs she makes are subpar. I've had far better from the gas station down the street." Mallory smirked, clearly satisfied with her remark.

Without even looking over my shoulder I stepped to my right, blocking Grandma Ruth from charging at Mallory. Grandma Ruth was fiercely loyal, and she wouldn't tolerate anyone talking badly about me.

"I'm sorry you feel that way, Mallory. I heard they're having a sale at the gas station today. Buy one, get one free on doughnuts, so perhaps you'd better get on over there before they're all gone," I said.

Grandma Ruth snickered from behind me. "Also, they don't sell éclairs at the gas station," she added.

"Anyway," Mallory sniffed, and she whipped a sheet of paper out from her bag. "I thought you might find this useful."

I took it hesitantly and skimmed it briefly. It was a list of potential improvements we might make around the bakery. Or, in her words, "necessary" improvements we "needed" to make around the bakery.

"Thank you," I said carefully, setting the list down. "But I think we're all right."

Mallory's mouth pursed into a small pucker and she took a deep breath. I resisted the urge to plug my ears in advance of her response, but before she could speak, a loud meow followed by a clatter came from the corner of the room. I turned around to see Pepper skittering across the counter and an overturned tray of croissants on the floor in his wake. We'd forgotten to shut the door to the kitchen and Pepper had swiftly taken advantage.

Grandma Ruth, with her stern expression I knew she'd mastered coaching from the sidelines of the football field, rushed over to the scene. She clearly had some pent-up aggression to let out after our confrontation with Mallory. She waved her rolling pin through the air like a red flag, indicating that Pepper should halt all activities and evacuate the kitchen.

"Scram!" she yelled, waving the rolling pin.

Pepper, startled by her loud orders, darted toward the counter like a player being told to drop and give her pushups. The cat knocked over a bag of flour in the process of fleeing the scene, and I winced.

"He's your fur kid, so you can clean up the mess," Grandma Ruth said with a scowl and a final wave of the rolling pin.

No doubt I'd have to spend a solid hour cleaning up the flour that now covered much of the bakery's kitchen.

"My phone," Mallory exclaimed frantically. "I had it just a moment ago, but now it's gone. Someone must have taken it!"

"Oh, well, I can help you look for it," I offered reluctantly, setting aside the broom.

"No, that won't be necessary. You need to focus on trying to bake better pastries," she said with a dismissive wave of her hand.

When I glanced back at Grandma Ruth, I saw her face turning redder by the second. Her face glowed with a ripe tomato redness and her eyes were almost closed, her mouth set in a kind of half sneer. *Uh-oh.* She was going to toss an éclair like a football at this woman if I didn't get her out of here fast.

"We'll make sure to keep an eye out for your missing phone," I said with a forced smile. The customer was always right, I reminded myself. Was she though? I shouldn't have to accept her insults.

"You probably hid my phone on purpose," Mallory said and then turned in a huff.

When Grandma Ruth picked up a nearby éclair from a tray, I grabbed her arm. "*Grandma.* We can't be throwing food at customers."

"She insulted you. She's been doing that all week and frankly, I've had enough," Grandma Ruth said, squinting tempestuously.

"She told me I should buy a new wardrobe because my clothes are hideous," Mr. Flannery said.

"She told me I should look into getting Botox," Mrs. Weston, one of our elderly patrons, said.

I hadn't seen Mrs. Weston approach but clearly, she had been standing here long enough to know who we were talking about. Meanwhile, Mallory hadn't left the bakery. Apparently, she was still searching for her missing phone. Her bad attitude continued to escalate. She started to pace around the café, muttering to herself and checking under tables. At least she was distracting the other customers from the explosion of flour and croissants that was going on behind the counter.

The bell over the door chimed as a tall, bald man entered the bakery and made a beeline for Mallory.

"Mallory, what are you doing?" he asked, his tone incredulous. "I thought you were just running to the ATM—I've been waiting in the car for fifteen minutes!"

Mallory turned toward the man, her eyes widening even further. "Thomas! Thank goodness you're here! I can't find my phone. I think *she* took it!"

She pointed in my direction. I grabbed Grandma Ruth's arm, not even looking over at her. Out of the corner of my eye, I'd seen her move for the éclairs again.

Thomas sighed and shook his head. "Mallory, I told you not to come here again. Honey, maybe you should take your medication."

But Mallory cut him off, her voice rising to a near shriek. "I need my phone! Check behind the counter—that *baker* probably took it!"

The other customers in the bakery had grown uncomfortable with the scene unfolding before them and started to edge toward the exit.

Thomas—maybe her husband?—shook his head slightly, but agreeably shifted over by the counter and peered over the edge, at the lower interior side of it where the cash register sat. I crossed my arms. They wouldn't find anything there. It was just the register, a cup of pens, a bowl of spare change for customers missing a couple pennies, and—

A cell phone in a bright red case.

Thomas and I jolted in surprise at the same moment, and he glanced up at me, a small frown creasing his forehead. "Oh," he said, and reached over to pick it up. He showed it to Mallory. "This one?"

My mouth dropped open just as Mallory snatched her phone and raised it triumphantly.

"See?" she exclaimed, waving it overhead. "Feeding customers cat hair *and* stealing phones!"

"Listen, I don't know how your phone got over there, but—"

"You can explain to the police," Mallory said snippily, and she tucked her phone into her purse. "I *won't* be returning to this establishment."

"I'm not getting my hopes up," Grandma Ruth muttered, and Mallory turned on her heel and strode out. The few remaining customers were murmuring among themselves, shiftily glancing over at Grandma Ruth and me. I threw my arms up, exasperated.

"That was an absolute disaster," I said, lowering my voice to talk just to Grandma Ruth. "Did you see how her phone got there? Did she *put* it there?"

"I was a bit distracted by your feral feline," Grandma Ruth said, and I wilted against the wall, all my energy evaporating. I still had to clean up all that flour.

Our small-town bakery was a cozy place, filled with the delicious aroma of freshly baked bread and pastries. I liked to think that it was a getaway from the stress of everyday life. But on this particular day, it seemed like a dark energy had settled over La Petite Patisserie. Mallory's black cloud of negativity had descended upon the shop like a monsoon, drenching every corner in her bleak attitude. Her scornful energy seemed to linger in the air and permeate every crevice with its heavy and oppressive malignancy, stifling the usual sense of coziness.

By the time I finished cleaning up after Pepper, a small group of locals had gathered by the counter, sipping their coffee and chatting with Grandma Ruth. As I got back to passing out orders, I overheard the customers discussing the latest gossip in town, all of which revolved around Mallory. She'd really made quite an impression in the few days since her arrival.

"I heard that new woman has been causing trouble again," said Mrs. Weston.

"Ugh, I can't stand her," chimed in Marcus, the carriage driver. "She's done nothing but stir up drama and make everyone miserable since she crossed the city limits."

I nodded in agreement, wiping my hands on my apron. "Yeah, I've had a few run-ins with her myself. She's not the nicest person, that's for sure."

The group continued to vent their frustrations about Mallory, each one sharing their own unpleasant experiences with her. I listened patiently, offering words of sympathy and commiseration. Thank goodness that after a while, the conversation turned to lighter topics. Soon the group began discussing their favorite bakery treats.

"I just love your petit fours," said Mrs. Weston. "They remind me of my honeymoon trip to Paris."

I smiled, pleased with the compliment. "Thank you. I'm so glad you like them."

As the group finished up their coffee and treats, they bid me goodbye and headed out into the sunshine. I watched them go, grateful for their company and happy to have been able to offer them a place to gather and chat. I just hoped Mallory hadn't scared anyone off from coming back. If customers thought they might have to deal with her again, then they might not return. I had been running the shop for a bit now and was just beginning to feel the satisfaction of having created something along with Grandma Ruth with our own hands and hard work. I had also become fond of the patrons who came by—the retirees who enjoyed leisurely conversations over coffee and cake, the families that gathered around the tables with their young children, the busy professionals who got their caffeine fix with a slice of something sweet on the side. All in addition to the usual flow of tourists.

As I cleaned up the tables and picked up the dishes, I couldn't help but keep thinking about Mallory and the negative energy she'd brought to town. Her husband had mentioned medication, so maybe her behavior was out of her control. Or perhaps she didn't realize how much her criticism was affecting people. Either way, I made a mental note to try and steer clear of Mallory in the future, and it seemed that the rest of the town would do the same.

A couple of quiet minutes passed, and I thought all the excitement for the day had ended. But as I was preparing a batch of fresh croissants, I looked up and saw a familiar face walking toward the counter.

It was Detective Ash. My heart skipped a beat as I watched him approach. I had to admit the truth—I had a bit of a crush on him. It wasn't like I knew him—it was like a celebrity crush. Harmless.

"Oh, no," I said, realizing why he was here. "Did Mallory actually call the police?"

Ash was trying not to laugh, I could see it in the wavering line of his mouth and the mirth in his eyes.

"Good morning, Madeline," Ash said, schooling his face into a stern expression. "I heard there was a theft."

As he looked around the now peaceful shop, I felt heat rush to my cheeks.

"I didn't actually steal her phone," I blurted.

"Maybe we should've," Grandma Ruth huffed.

"It's just—Pepper knocked over a batch of croissants, and a bag of flour, and when I turned back around, Mallory's phone was—" I waved at the business side of the counter. "I don't know how it got there, but—"

Ash raised his hands, and his face finally broke into a grin. "Don't worry," he said. "I know neither of you are the type to commit petty theft. Or at least, I think you'd probably do it a bit more effectively than just setting a phone down a couple feet away from your victim." He said the latter half of his statement while eying Grandma Ruth, who twiddled her thumbs innocently.

"Listen, next time Mallory comes by, just give me a call, all right? I've been hearing all kinds of stories about her since she got to town," Ash continued. "She's not here to make friends, that's for sure."

"Here to make enemies, more like," Grandma Ruth added, and I waved her off. Best not to dig too deep a hole in case the next accusation from Mallory had any more heft to it.

"Right. Well, I'm glad everything is okay now," Ash said, and he leaned against the counter, eying the pastry case. "Since I'm here, maybe I can get a coffee and a pastry?"

"Of course!" I replied, trying to hide my excitement. "What can I get for you? I'm guessing you want a spandauer?"

Ash looked over the menu board before answering. "How about a mocha and. . . . a *pain au chocolat*?" He said the last bit carefully, as if sounding out the words.

I was pleasantly surprised at his selection—and by his sweet tooth. I quickly got to work, trying my best to act normal, even though I was thoroughly flustered by the entire situation . . . and by having a handsome man watching me steam milk.

Our fingers brushed as I handed him his cup, and I winced, sure that my every thought was written across my face. I wasn't exactly a natural at romance—my friends back in LA would be telling me to just ask him to go to dinner, or at least to *flirt* and get him to ask me to dinner. Best I could do was turn bright red and avoid eye contact. Ash smiled softly as he took the cup, raising it to his mouth and taking a small sip.

"Thanks, Madeline," Ash said, breaking the brief moment of silence between us. "Your grandma and grandpa always made the best espresso. I see you inherited the gene."

"It's on me this morning. Since you were nice enough to come by and not arrest me."

"You don't have to do that. I can pay."

"I insist," I said.

As Ash turned to leave, I couldn't help but watch him go, admiring the way he moved with quiet confidence.

"I know seeing him has made your day. He's a fine-looking man. Now you'll be thinking about him for the rest of the day," Grandma Ruth said.

"Grandma, oh my gosh," I muttered, dropping my head in my hands. "I can't believe he actually came by here about that stupid phone."

"Solvang isn't exactly a hotbed for criminal activity," Grandma Ruth said. "But, you know, he might've come by for another reason."

"I'm sure you mean the delicious pastries," I said, pursing my lips at her.

She raised her pale eyebrows. "Sure."

"I'm too busy right now to even think about a love life," I told her.

"Weren't you seeing someone back in LA? You were just as busy back then and managed to find the time."

"This is a different kind of busy right now and that wasn't anything serious. Just a couple of dates." I did sometimes find myself thinking of James, the sommelier. He'd been disappointed when I'd told him I was relocating to open up my own business, but we hadn't been truly *involved*. We'd kept in light touch over social media, with him promising to come visit the bakery someday. But I knew Solvang might as well be in the remote wilderness to sophisticated Angelenos like him.

"Life can't be all work and no play, Madeline," Grandma Ruth admonished. "Sometimes I worry you're letting the business take over your life."

"Well, that may be true but right now, I have actual work to do." With that, I turned and headed for the kitchen, letting Grandma Ruth know the topic was over for now.

Chapter Five

The bell over the bakery door jingled merrily as an awkward, shaggy-haired teenager stumbled inside. His eyes roved around, eagerly taking in the displays of baked goods and the warmth of fresh baked bread and pastry. The sleeves of his white T-shirt were snug, trapping his arms tightly. His shirt seemed to grow tighter with each passing moment, and he fidgeted with its hem until he approached the counter. In contrast, his jeans were baggy and too big. I couldn't believe that was back in style, having lived through it during my own teen years.

"Bonjour! How can I help you?" I asked, greeting him with a friendly smile.

The teenager cleared his throat before replying. "Um, I'm just looking around."

"Well, let me know if you want to try anything. I'm happy to give you a sample."

He stared for a moment at a cake I'd frosted earlier that day and topped with a variety of delicate sugar flowers. "Do you like flowers?" he asked rather abruptly.

Well, I hadn't expected that.

I raised my eyebrows. "Flowers? I mean, sure I do . . . but why?"

The teenager shifted from one foot to the other. "I thought I might buy some for you. I just wanted to show you how much I admire you. I think you're really beautiful."

"That's very sweet of you, but I'm afraid I'm a bit too old for you. Have we met before?"

"My name is Frankie Castille. I plan on attending the California State University this fall," he said. "And I just think it would be great if you could go out with me."

I recognized the name—my grandma lived next door to the Castilles.

"I really am flattered, but I'm just your friendly neighborhood baker, not someone you should be thinking of in that way."

The teenager's face turned red, and he looked down at his feet. "Oh, I didn't mean to make things awkward. I just thought that maybe—"

"It's okay," I interrupted gently.

Frankie nodded, his eyes still fixed on the floor. "I'm sorry. I'll go now."

I reached out and touched his arm. "Hey, don't feel bad. You're a good kid, and I appreciate the gesture. But sometimes, things just don't work out the way we want them to. It's nothing personal."

Frankie stared at me for a moment. "Thanks for understanding. Maybe I'll come back another time for some dessert."

I nodded and watched as he left the shop, feeling a mix of sympathy and relief. I knew that dealing with teenagers was part of the job since they sometimes came in before and after school, but I never thought one would ask me on a date. Thank goodness Grandma Ruth hadn't overheard that exchange. She'd surely make fun of me for that.

The afternoon sun streamed through the front windows of the bakery, illuminating the room with a warm, golden light. The window display was an oasis of sweet treats that beckoned to passersby with its colorful display. Domed pastries glistened behind the thick glass of the cases—glazed, sugared, and sprinkled with nuts, each one a confectionary masterpiece. My artfully crafted muffins and cookies were like precious jewels in paper wrappings, while the delectable loaves of bread resting in their baskets filled the air with a homey aroma. Tarts, éclairs, and macarons added a bright sparkle to the room. As always, the sweet scent of baking bread and cakes filled the air. I surveyed the shop with satisfaction, remembering the hard work that had gone into rejuvenating the business.

"Should we go shopping for a dress?" Grandma Ruth asked.

I spun around and clutched my chest. "Oh, Ruth, I didn't hear you back there. Shopping for a dress? For what?"

"For prom, of course," Grandma Ruth said with a straight face.

"So you were back there and heard." I sighed.

"Oh, I heard it all," she said.

"That was so awkward," I said helplessly. "Teenagers are so weird."

"Frankie has always seemed like a decent kid." Grandma Ruth leaned against the counter. "Keeps quiet and mostly to himself. He seems innocent enough, right? I seem to remember you having a crush on our postman when you were a kid."

"Oh my gosh," I said, the memory flooding back. "I was such a weird kid! Don't remind me."

"You handled it well, anyway."

"Yeah. Hopefully he moves on to someone more age appropriate," I said, cringing imagining having to deal with awkward teenage advances again if he didn't drop it.

Grandma Ruth nodded slowly. "You want me to talk to his parents about it?"

I shook my head and laughed. "No. Can you imagine? I would've just died if that mailman had told my parents when I left a valentine for him in the mailbox when I was ten."

"Oh, I told them."

"*Grandma*!"

Chapter Six

A few days had passed, and all was once again quiet and peaceful in Solvang. Though there remained a gnawing in my stomach that made me feel as if a storm was brewing. Grandma Ruth and I stood in the waiting area of town hall, a quaint building with wooden beams and a shingled roof. It looked more like a cottage than a municipal building. The baking contest would commence in just a few minutes. The chatter of the small crowd was high with excitement; it was like a beehive of people swarming and calling out to one another as they waited for the contest to begin.

The host and MC was Suzette Abbott, a local real estate agent and a member of the city council. Suzette made her way through the crowd, welcoming each contestant by name and wishing them luck with their entries. Her voice boomed through the room, professional and clear. She wore a tailored pin-striped skirt and blazer, outlining her slender waist and narrow shoulders. Her short black hair curled at her chin and gleamed in the sunlight coming through the window.

Already the smell of cinnamon and sugar wafted through the air. My stomach flipped as I thought about what I had gotten myself into. I'd entered the contest, so now I had to face the possibility of failure. I wasn't sure how well this would go since I wasn't in the comfort of my own kitchen.

I looked around the room to survey my competition in the baking contest. Mrs. Spencer had brought ingredients to bake her chocolate chip cookies, which Grandma Ruth told me were beloved at every church function. Surprisingly I spied cayenne pepper on Mrs. Spencer's tray. Artie Smothers had everything ready to bake her infamous lemon pie. I'd heard via the local gossip that the one she'd entered into the pie contest at the county fair had been so tart that it acted like a seal for the mouth after one bite, making it almost impossible to unpucker for a solid minute.

Mrs. Castille and her teenage son, Frankie, briefly stopped by my station as they headed to join the crowd of spectators.

"Good luck, Madeline," Mrs. Castille said cheerfully.

"We're rooting for you," Frankie added with a shy smile before hurrying off to follow his mother.

I didn't even have time to thank them for their support before I felt fresh eyes on me. When I looked over, I spotted Natalie Simms headed my way. Natalie worked at one of the traditional Danish bakeries in town. We'd first met when I was doing some research by sampling the local fare and discovered we shared a passion for baking. Even though we were technically competitors, she'd only ever been sweet to me, helpful in sharing information about the local business and complimentary toward my baked goods. But I'd never seen Natalie like this before. Her usually cheerful demeanor was replaced by a fierce glare that could rival a storm cloud. Tensions were already high in the room, but Natalie's anger caught me off guard.

She marched over, her face flushed with fury, and I felt the heat of her anger coming from her body. "Madeline!" Her voice sliced through the air, sharp and cutting.

I turned, startled by the intensity of her anger. Lately it felt like the whole town was out to confront me. "Natalie, what's wrong?" I tried to keep my tone calm, but her anger was palpable.

"You! You know exactly what's wrong," she hissed, her fingers trembling with frustration.

My mind raced, trying to pinpoint what I might have done to provoke this from a woman I considered to be a friendly peer. "Natalie, I honestly don't know what you're talking about," I replied.

She scoffed, shaking her head in disbelief. "You sabotaged my bake! Don't play innocent with me. You took some of my ingredients. I saw you by my table a while ago."

Sabotage? The accusation hit me like a splash of cold water. "Natalie, I'd never do that!" I protested, feeling hurt and bewildered by her accusation. "Why would I?"

Her eyes flashed with resentment. "Because you're jealous! You can't stand seeing others succeed, can you?" Her voice wavered with a mix of anger and hurt.

"I don't know what you're talking about," I said, trying to keep my voice steady. "I would never do something like that."

She seemed torn between rage and disbelief, her breaths coming in quick, agitated gasps. "This is ridiculous. You're always acting like you're so above us, coming from a big city and doing everything the fancy French way. And now you're trying to ruin this for me."

I felt the eyes of the room on us, the tension in the room escalating. Natalie's accusation hung heavily between us, and

I felt a pang of hurt at her words. "I didn't touch your stuff, Natalie," I said firmly, my voice tinged with hurt. "I hope you find out what happened, but it wasn't me."

She turned abruptly, storming away, leaving me feeling shaken and confused. The weight of her accusation lingered in the air, and I couldn't shake off the sting of her anger. I'd never imagined Natalie could get so angry and I was left reeling from the confrontation, wondering how things had gone so wrong. Then my eyes landed on someone I hadn't expected to see in the crowd: Mallory. What was *she* doing here? I had a feeling if we got close enough to each other sparks would fly between us like an electrical storm. Had she come because she had heard I had entered the contest? A restless energy buzzed through me.

As soon as Mallory spotted me, her nose wrinkled in distaste and now she was headed my way. Thank goodness Grandma Ruth had stepped away for a minute. Otherwise, baked goods would have been hurtling through the air like mini weapons. A chaotic food fight would erupt, with a few fists thrown in too. I watched in anticipation as Mallory drew near. She walked over to my tray of éclair ingredients and surveyed it all with her usual critical eye.

Mallory's outfit was effortlessly chic. Whatever issues she had, the woman knew how to dress. It was the kind of ensemble that screamed understated luxury. She wore a tailored camel-colored jacket with a high collar, cinched at the waist with a leather belt that matched her glossy knee-high boots. Underneath, a cream silk blouse peeked out, its delicate ruffles adding a soft contrast to the structured jacket. Her slim, beige trousers were perfectly pressed, the sharp creases running down to her boots as though she'd just stepped off a runway. Dangling gold earrings glinted beneath her perfectly styled hair, and a black leather handbag with a discreet designer logo completed the look. Even in the muted tones, she stood out like a beacon of sophistication.

"I notice that you haven't put much effort into your ingredients. It looks like they were bought from a discount store," Mallory said with a smirk.

What could I say in return? There was no way would I stoop to her level, so I just remained silent.

Mallory pulled out a container of sugar from her large tote bag. "I brought only the best for my entry." Not only was she in a designer outfit, but she had apparently also entered the contest and brought along expensive, imported ingredients too. If she was a baker herself, that helped explain some of her hypercritical behavior toward me. But she was hardly dressed for baking in her chic ensemble. Mallory snorted in disdain as she glared out at the room full of bakers. "These people are all amateurs. I'll win easily." With a final smug look she turned and walked away.

I watched as she began to set up her station. Mallory made sure to keep a wide berth from the other contestants. Maybe she didn't want to catch any of their "common" baking habits. Mallory noticed me looking at her and gave me another smirk before confidently smiling at the judges sitting at a table across the room. I gritted my teeth and tried to stay focused on my own creation, made with fresh ingredients from my own kitchen. The most expensive ingredients weren't needed for great taste. I just hoped it would be enough to beat Mallory. I had no idea what her skills were like in the kitchen, but she certainly talked a big game.

The space was small and crowded, but I managed to maneuver around it without too much difficulty. The sun was shining through the window behind me, and outside I heard the birds chirping. Yet my heart was beating faster, as I hoped that the sweet treat I was about to create would turn out great.

I brought the water, French butter, sugar, and salt to a boil in a medium saucepan before stirring in the flour with a wooden spoon, watching as the dough came together and started to form a ball. I then transferred the dough to a bowl and added the eggs one at a time, stirring until they were fully incorporated.

Next, I filled a pastry bag with the dough and piped it onto a baking sheet, forming logs that would become the exquisite final product. I placed the baking sheet into the hot oven, taking care not to disturb the delicate logs. While the dough was baking, I prepared the chocolate icing, melting down chocolate in a small pot with a bit of cream.

It was difficult to focus on my work; the baking contest wasn't a haven of sweet aromas and camaraderie. It seemed on the brink of a chaotic showdown. Several contestants, each meticulously focused on their baking stations, couldn't seem to shake off a brewing dispute. In the corner of the room, Abigail Price exchanged heated whispers with Morgan Whitmore, a competitive baker with a penchant for show-stopping cakes. Their spat had started over an oven timer but had quickly escalated.

"You're hogging the oven, Abigail! I need to get my cake in!" Morgan barked, his tone filled with irritation.

"You've got to wait your turn, Morgan! We all have the same time limit here," Abigail retorted, her patience clearly wearing thin.

On the other side of the kitchen, Sylvia, whom Grandma Ruth had told me was known for her precision, squared off against Liam, an ambitious newcomer with a flair for inventive desserts. Their debate was about counter space, and it had turned into a full-blown argument.

"You're encroaching on my area, Sylvia! Move your things!" Liam demanded, pointing at Sylvia's ingredients spilling onto his workspace.

Sylvia replied sharply, "Watch your own station, Liam! You're in my way too!"

As the competition continued, the animosity among the contestants heightened. The clatter of utensils and the sound of raised voices filled the air, disrupting the atmosphere of the contest.

The judges, sensing the escalating tension, stepped in, attempting to calm the situation.

"Contestants, let's keep it civil. Remember, it's about the baking," Suzette called out, trying to diffuse the mounting tension. The room quieted, but the tense glares continued to ricochet around the room as the oven timers ticked away.

The aroma emanating from the ovens was intoxicating, and my anticipation grew as the minutes ticked by. Finally, my timer dinged, and I removed my beautiful creations from the oven. I inhaled their heavenly scent. I let them cool before piping in the cream and then drizzling on the chocolate icing. The sight of the finished product stirred something within me, and I savored the moment, feeling a deep sense of accomplishment. Éclairs were a classic dessert, especially with their thick pastry cream filling.

As the judges made their way around the room, I held my breath and crossed my fingers. I was nervous when they finally reached Mallory's table. I watched them as they sampled her entry. I couldn't tell what she had prepared, as I was too far away to see.

"What did Mallory enter into the contest?" I asked Grandma as she walked up. She'd been wandering around the room checking out the competition.

When she didn't answer, I glanced over at her. She had a funny look on her face. Why wasn't she answering me?

"What is it that you don't want to tell me?" I asked.

Finally, Grandma Ruth said, "Mallory made éclairs."

"What? Why would she do that?" I narrowed my eyes and stared in Mallory's direction.

She must have felt my glare because she looked over at me and smirked.

"Don't worry, there's no way they're as good as yours. You have nothing to worry about. You've got this," Grandma Ruth said.

I tried to believe her words, but I couldn't help but have some doubts. I was good at what I did, but I couldn't be too confident. No doubt Mallory would have something bad to say about my éclairs. I vowed to try and avoid her and thereby also avoid a confrontation.

My hands trembled as I carefully slid my éclairs from the cooling rack onto a serving platter. I stepped back and assessed their appearance. They weren't quite as perfect as I had hoped, but I reminded myself that it was my first time baking in a contest, and my hands hadn't been as steady as they usually were. I could only hope they would be good enough.

As I watched the judges slowly make their way over to my station, I took a deep breath and steeled myself. No matter what happened, I knew I had done my best.

"Well, it's showtime," I said. I hoped this would prove to Mallory that she had no idea what she was talking about when she said my baked goods were subpar.

Grandma Ruth had wandered off toward the judges' table. I watched as she cast a glance around. My eyebrows furrowed in confusion. I was torn between curiosity and unease as Grandma Ruth lingered near the table. Her back was facing me now and I couldn't make out exactly what she was doing. Was she up to something or just being curious?

"Grandma Ruth, what are you doing?" I whispered when she returned, trying to keep my voice casual, despite the disquiet in my mind.

"Oh, nothing, just looking around," she replied, trying to sound nonchalant.

Was she trying to be sneaky and tip the scales in my favor? I couldn't decide. Grandma Ruth had always been an honest person, on and off the football field, but apparently this contest had brought out the competitive edge in everyone.

"Okay, just make sure it's not something that might affect the outcome of the contest," I said, trying to give her the benefit of the doubt.

She smiled widely. "Of course not, dear."

As I turned my focus back to my éclairs, a lingering doubt remained in my mind. Grandma Ruth's actions seemed harmless, but in the heat of competition, even the most innocent gestures could become suspect. I decided to let the judges do their jobs and handle everything.

The smell of fresh baked goodies was still thick in the air. All the contestants had baked their best recipes, hoping to win the grand prize. I prayed my recipe would make the judges drool. Despite the sour looks from Mallory and some of the other contestants, I did my best to appear unfazed by their scrutiny. Frankie and Mrs. Castille waved from the audience. I pushed my shoulders back and placed a big smile on my face.

As the judges continued to make their rounds, my confidence level wavered. One minute I was sure that my éclairs would blow away the competition, and the next I thought for sure they'd hate them.

The judges hadn't shown any signs of preference as they'd taken a bite from each contestant's entry. Finally, it was my turn. I was the very last contestant to be judged. Would I be able to read what they were thinking when they tasted my éclairs? As they stood in front of the plate of éclairs, all but one of them smiled broadly. When they tasted my entry, their faces remained impassive. My heart sank until I heard one of them speak.

"Wow," one of the judges said, holding up one of my éclairs.

"Mm, this is delicious!" another exclaimed.

"I love the level of sweetness and the texture," another added.

A surge of pride and relief swept over me. My hard work had paid off! And I'd done it without the expensive ingredients Mallory had boasted about earlier.

As I tried to absorb what was happening as a few of the other contestants approached my station.

"Those look amazing," one of them said. "I wish I could bake like you."

Mallory, however, stood off to the side, scowling. I tried not to let her behavior bother me, but I couldn't help feeling confusion over her continued animosity. It was like she had set out to dislike me from the day she'd first entered the bakery.

Thoughts of Mallory soon faded as the judges prepared to announce the winner. A nervous flutter tightened in my stomach in anticipation as they listed off the runners-up, until finally—

"And the winner of our inaugural bakeoff—Madeline Andersen!"

I heard a smattering of whoops among the polite applause, and I firmly avoided eye contact with Mallory as I was guided up to the stage to receive my trophy. I wasn't sure if I was expected to make a speech or not, but I wasn't going to blow the opportunity for some free publicity for the bakery. So after a photographer snapped a photo of me holding the trophy alongside the judges, I piped up:

"Thank you all so much for this honor, and for welcoming me back to Solvang so sweetly! If you'd like a further taste of our éclairs and more, be sure to come visit us at La Petit Patisserie!"

The crowd applauded, and Grandma Ruth gave a mighty whoop. I felt like I was on top of the world. But Mallory quickly made her presence known. She walked up to me as I stepped down from the stage. Her movements were graceful, but her expression was cold.

"Congratulations," she said, her voice smooth as silk, yet laced with an underlying resentment that I recognized all too well. She paused before adding, "Obviously the contest was rigged. I'll have to find a way to prove it."

I knew she was trying to hide her insecurity behind a veneer of superiority. I could sense the deep-seated envy in her words. So I simply smiled and nodded, knowing that my éclairs had been wonderful and trophy-worthy.

She stared at me as if expecting a greater response. I didn't want to further our animosity, but I also didn't want to back down.

"Thanks, but the contest was clearly on the up-and-up," I said, trying to keep my voice even. "This was a recipe I've been refining for a long time."

At that, Mallory just snorted and walked away. I couldn't help feeling a little sad that a fellow baker couldn't be happy for me, but I wouldn't let her dampen my spirits. I had won fair and square, and that was something to be proud of.

But Mallory wasn't finished yet. She stormed over to the judges and barked, "What about my éclairs? Did you not notice how delicious they are?" Her voice was full of anger.

One of the judges cleared his throat. "They were quite good . . . but not the best," he said simply.

"Good?" Mallory's voice rose in disbelief. "What do you mean, good? They are perfect! They are masterpieces! They are miles ahead of anything else in this contest! Especially hers." She gestured toward me.

The judges exchanged uncomfortable glances. "Well, we appreciate your enthusiasm, but we've made our decision and that's final," Suzette said.

Mallory's face turned red with anger. "That's it? That's all you have to say? You're just saying that because you're intimidated by my talent! You wouldn't know an éclair if it hit you in the face!"

Mallory rushed away, a fury in her steps similar to the day in the bakery when she'd been looking for her phone. Soon her stare landed on me. Her gaze blazed with anger. She clenched her fists at her sides and marched back over to me, slamming her fist on the table next to us. I noticed that she had left a piece of paper on the table. Was it another list of insults directed toward me? A passive-aggressive list of ways I should improve? But on the paper was a neatly written recipe for éclairs.

"Does this look familiar to you?" she demanded, pointing to the paper.

I looked from the paper back to Mallory, my face surely displaying my puzzlement. "I'm sorry, but is that supposed to mean something to me?" I asked warily.

"You stole my éclair recipe!" Mallory seethed. "I know it's mine! You are a thief!"

A few of the people lingering in the room gasped in shock. My eyes widened with fright. I had no idea Mallory would become this unhinged over a small-town baking contest. I considered handing over the trophy just so she'd leave me alone.

"I can assure you I have never seen this recipe before. As a pastry chef, I create all of my recipes from scratch."

"Don't lie to me!" Mallory hissed. "I've been perfecting this recipe for years. It's my grandmother's secret recipe, and you stole it from me and claimed it as your own. I demand an explanation!"

I reflexively clutched my trophy tighter to my chest. I'd changed my mind. No way would I hand over my trophy to this deranged woman. She'd have to pry it out of my cold, dead hands. I glowered at her as she now stood inches from my face. Her jaw was tightly clenched and her eyes narrowed. I backed up a couple steps and tried to prepare myself in case she decided to throw a punch at me.

"I swear I didn't take your recipe," I said, trying to defuse the situation. "It's just a coincidence that it's similar. Look, you can see my notes if you want."

Mallory's expression didn't soften. Not even slightly. I put the trophy down and grabbed my bag. I pulled out my book of recipes. I carried it around with me almost everywhere

I went so I could jot down notes and bits of inspiration as they struck. The thick notebook filled with recipes accumulated over the course of several years was one of my most prized possessions.

"Here, this is my recipe development journal," I said, flipping through the pages various recipes I had worked up. I finally found my recipe for éclairs and pointed at it. "See?"

Mallory studied the page for a few seconds before looking up at me with unapologetic eyes.

"That proves nothing. You could have faked it."

"That makes no sense! Why would I do that? And furthermore, where would I have even found your recipe?" I asked.

"You're sneaky. I'm sure you have your ways," she snapped.

The judges and crowd looked on incredulously. I hadn't expected this to escalate into such a scene. Whispers filled the space as the spectators exchanged nervous glances, unsure whether to intervene or let the dramatic scene play out. From across the room, I heard Liam and Sylvia's poorly muffled arguing again. Liam was accusing her of causing him to lose the competition.

I sighed and placed my recipe book back into my bag. "Look, I can understand why you're upset because you wanted to win, but I swear to you, I didn't steal your recipe. It's just a coincidence that you think it's similar to yours. Why don't we just put this behind us?"

Mallory glared at me, her fists clenched. "When I get the proof that you're lying, you'll regret it."

I realized that she really wasn't going to let this go. I glanced over my shoulder and spotted Grandma Ruth approaching.

"What seems to be the problem?" Grandma Ruth asked in a clipped tone.

"It's fine, Ruth. We should leave now." I tried to guide Grandma Ruth away, but I might as well have tried to move a linebacker. It wasn't happening. She wasn't budging.

Mallory puffed out her chest. "You think I'm afraid of you? I'm not."

"You should be," Grandma Ruth snapped.

"She stole my éclair recipe," Mallory yelled.

"What? That's crazy," Grandma Ruth said. "And I don't appreciate you talking to my grandaughter like that."

"Too bad, old lady," Mallory said.

"You'd better watch your step, Mallory, or you'll be sorry. I'll see to that," Grandma Ruth said, stepping closer to Mallory.

"Grandma. Just let it go." I grabbed Grandma Ruth's arm and attempted to pull her back.

In a sudden swoop, Mallory snatched up my trophy and took off running. Grandma Ruth picked up the first thing at hand, which happened to be one of my éclairs, and hurled it at Mallory, hitting her squarely in the back of the head. Years of throwing footballs on the field had made her an expert shot.

The next thing I knew, chaos erupted in the town hall. Mallory retaliated by grabbing a nearby sponge cake and flinging it in our direction. Desserts were suddenly flying everywhere. Pies and cakes, custards and éclairs and cookies—nothing was safe from the food fight. I tried to find a place to hide, but there was no escape. It seemed like everyone was now involved; no one was spared. All of the pent-up aggression from earlier in the contest had erupted. Grandma Ruth and Mallory were at the center of things, fighting tooth and nail, throwing anything they could get their hands on at one another.

Suddenly, someone yelled out, “Stop!”

Everyone stopped what they were doing and looked up to see who had spoken. It was Ash. I couldn’t have been more embarrassed as I stood with a blueberry pie in my hand, ready to toss it. He stood there with his hands on his hips, his face stern as he surveyed the damage done. I wasn’t sure if he’d been in attendance the whole time or had been summoned once things got heated between Mallory and me.

“What is going on here? This is supposed to be a baking contest, not a battlefield!” Ash chided.

“Madeline didn’t cheat,” Grandma Ruth announced quietly as she wiped whipped topping from her cheek. “She deserves the trophy.”

Ash looked around at all of us in bewilderment. After what felt like forever, Ash sighed heavily, and said, “If none of you wants disorderly charges, you’ll help clean all this up. And return the trophy to whoever actually won.”

Mallory grudgingly handed over my trophy before Ash began to quickly clear everyone who wasn’t actively red-handed with frosting and jam out of the town hall. At least I’d gotten the trophy back. But now we had a mess to clean up. Mallory had strolled out of the building, leaving a trail of crumbs with every step she took.

“Nice shot, Ruth,” I whispered. “That éclair hit her right in the back of the head.”

Grandma Ruth just snickered.

Chapter Seven

I'd placed my trophy in the front window of the bakery. Throughout the day customers had commented on it and congratulated me for the win. Of course there was also some talk about the fight that had broken out. I'd never hear the end of that. There had been no sign of Mallory, though. I knew I should take comfort in that, but I had a feeling she would show up soon. I hadn't talked to Ash yet either. Though I thought about hiding from him due to embarrassment, I supposed I couldn't avoid him forever.

After a long day of work, Grandma Ruth and I made our way to the back door. We'd stayed until dark working on a catering order, but it was finally done. Grandma Ruth had gotten to do some good ranting and venting about Mallory without any customers in the bakery, especially after we'd seen her walk by the front of the store not once, not twice, but three times, the last of which being only twenty minutes ago, when Mallory paused outside the glass, illuminated by the streetlights as she peered at us before she bustled along.

Grandma Ruth stepped out the back door to leave just as I spotted a lone tray of croissants that we'd forgotten to box up for the catering job.

"You go on—I'll take care of these before I lock up."

"Are you sure?"

"Go on, I know you have bridge tonight with your friends. I'll be fine."

"See you in the morning then, sugar," Grandma Ruth said as she headed off.

I focused on finishing up, arranging the croissants into white boxes and tying them closed with pink string. The bakery was totally silent, devoid of customers, Grandma Ruth, and even Pepper, whom I had left at home. So I was jolted when there was a strange noise. It was a loud, scraping sound coming from somewhere in the alleyway. I cracked open the back door and peered through. But since it was dark out I couldn't see all the way down the alleyway. Was someone down there? My eyes widened with fear.

I tried to tell myself it was probably just a cat. But it would have to be a pretty big cat. Or a rat the size of a cat. I eased away from the back door and took a few steps down the alleyway toward the dumpster, trying to stay as quiet as possible. I made sure to grab my phone from the counter before stepping out and gripped it tightly in my hand. Out of the corner of my eye, I thought I saw—or sensed—movement around the side of the building at the end of the alley. I hesitated, unsure of what to do. Should I call the police? And tell them—what?—that I saw a flutter of movement?

I stared down the alleyway, watching in case the figure returned. It was hard to make out many details in the darkness, but it had seemed to be large enough to be a person and not an animal. Instinct took over and I ran forward, away from the bakery's back door and toward the end of the alley where it met the street. I'd figure out what to do once I was safely outside the alley on the well-lit sidewalk. I half turned my head to keep an eye on anything behind me when I ran smack into something—something large and warm. A person's back.

"Ruth! I thought you'd left!"

My relief at seeing her turned icy at the sight of her face as she turned to look at me. She looked dazed and glassy-eyed. There was a bundled object directly in front of her on the ground.

"What's going on?" I asked, grabbing her arm.

"I . . . I left, but then saw someone had left a trash bag on the ground near the dumpster down the way. I was worried about rats so I went and grabbed it and threw it away." Her normally confident voice was hushed and uncertain. "I heard something behind me, but when I turned around there was nothing. Then I saw another trash bag on the ground. Only . . . only it wasn't trash. It's . . ."

"Oh my God," I gasped, taking a step back. I pulled out my phone and shined its flashlight on the form. "It's *Mallory* . . ."

Mallory was on the ground, lying in a small pool of her own blood near her head, her eyes open but fixed in an empty stare of death. It was clear from the lack of movement and her pale, lifeless skin that Mallory was dead.

"We—oh my gosh. We have to call the police," I said.

Grandma Ruth just nodded, clearly still in shock as I dialed. I'd never had to report a dead body before, so I just told them that there had been a terrible accident and to come as quickly as possible. The 911 operator stayed eerily calm on the other line, peppering me with questions and encouraging me to stay on the line.

When I'd first spotted Mallory, I assumed she'd had some sort of accident, that she'd fallen and hit her head or had some sort of medical episode. But when I caught the words "potential assault" from the 911 operator my thoughts were flung in a new and even worse direction.

"Was she . . . was she attacked? Killed?" I wasn't sure if I was asking the phone operator, Grandma Ruth or myself. Maybe all three of us. "Who could do something like this?" I asked, not expecting her to answer.

My heart thumped against my chest as I leaned closer to Mallory's body, unable to believe that this had happened. But there was no denying it. She was gone. Another chill ran down my spine as I realized how close we had been to the murderer. Mallory had been on the sidewalk mere minutes earlier. The killer must have been waiting somewhere nearby. Just moments before she'd been complaining to me, and now she was gone forever. The last thing I'd expected was to find her murdered in the alleyway behind my shop. Maybe if I hadn't insisted she leave, she'd still be alive. But there was no changing it now. Mallory's fate was sealed, and all I could do was stand in shock and try to comprehend this tragedy. It was a stark reminder that danger could be lurking anywhere, even in our own neighborhood.

Police lights flashed on the alley walls and, seconds later, the police descended into the alleyway like a swarm of bees, their presence immediately saturating the air with an even more oppressive sense of dread. Grandma Ruth and I stood over the dead body, her expression stoic and unreadable as they approached. I felt my stomach drop as it hit me that from their perspective, they'd just walked up on us standing over the dead body of a woman we'd been publicly feuding with. It didn't look good.

I thought back to Mallory and me arguing right before she was killed—had anyone seen us just now? Certainly everyone had seen us fight at the competition. Would the police think I or Grandma Ruth could be responsible for her death? The fear of being arrested for something I hadn't done began to consume me. I watched silently as the police moved around the alley, hovering over the body, taking notes and photographs for evidence. They seemed to slowly be closing in on us, trapping us with their overwhelming presence until I felt as if I might end up in handcuffs.

"Do you think they'll arrest me?" Grandma Ruth asked.

"Of course not. I don't think so," I said sounding less confident. "I mean, I hope not."

Rain had started to fall around us now, a dreary, relentless patter that seemed to take on a malevolent life of its own. The crime scene suddenly felt even tenser, the darkness of the night enhanced by the dancing drops of moisture.

Eventually, Grandma Ruth was taken off to the side by a couple of officers so they could interview us separately. I was left standing by myself in the alley. Even though there was no one talking to me at the moment, I still felt the pressure of their eyes on me. Were they judging me and silently accusing me of something I hadn't done? Anxiety rippled through my veins like a shockwave, leaving me trembling in its wake.

A few seconds later, Detective Ash strode onto the crime scene. His handsome face was set in a stony expression, and his piercing eyes missed nothing. He scrutinized every detail of the surroundings, as if he could divine some clue from the dumpster or the brick walls. With his arrival, it now seemed the entire police force had assembled at the scene. All of them seemingly knowing exactly what they were doing while I remained clueless. It was easy to see by his confidence and movements why Ash was in charge. He stepped forward, his feet making no noise on the pavement. He stopped in front of the body, his eyes sweeping the area. Everyone stood still and silent, watching him. He started giving out commands.

"Let's start looking for evidence on the other side streets too," he said, his voice coming out in a low rumble. "We need to find out what happened here."

And so they began, the search for answers slowly unfolding beneath the dark veil of the night. As I stood there in shock, I couldn't help but look around at my surroundings. It was just in my nature to want answers too. The detectives weren't the only ones who wanted to find a clue. The gravity of what had happened made me want to find out who had done this right away.

Grandma Ruth stood like a statue farther up the alley, listening to something the police were saying to her. I wasn't so sedentary, though. I fidgeted from one foot to the other and wandered down the alleyway toward the dumpster. No one stopped me, so I figured it was okay. I peeked around the dumpster. What was I even looking for? The bag of garbage Grandma Ruth had said she'd thrown away? Did that mean I didn't fully trust her story? Within seconds, my eyes narrowed in on something glinting on the ground. My heart skipped a beat as I inched closer and saw that it was a key fob. The logo on the front indicated that it was for a Toyota. Could it be evidence?

Leaning down, I examined the key fob more closely. It was small and silver, with a few scratches and dings on the surface. I wasn't about to touch that key fob, though. The last thing I wanted was my fingerprints on a piece of evidence from the crime scene. I scanned the rest of the alley. It was narrow, with tall walls on either side. There were no windows, and the only source of light was coming from a single streetlight near the entrance. I looked around for any other clues, but all I could find was an empty bottle, some broken glass, and a few cigarette butts.

As crazy as it seemed, I decided to look inside the dumpster itself. Grandma Ruth still stood motionless as the police asked her questions. The rest of the police were too wrapped up in looking at the body to pay attention to me, apparently clueless as to what I was doing. I covered my fingers with my sleeve, flipped the lid of the dumpster open, and peered inside. The stench was overwhelming, and I had to cover my nose with my shirt to keep from gagging. There were piles of trash everywhere, but nothing that looked like evidence.

Just as I was about to give up on finding anything else, I noticed something tucked between two bags of garbage. It was a white recipe card. Pretty little cherries were printed on the top. I carefully reached in and pulled it out, pinched between my fingers covered by the fabric of my shirt. I took the card over to the streetlight and got a better look at it. I knew the recipe card wasn't one of mine, but I wasn't sure what I'd found. I jumped when a voice came directly at my ear:

"Madeline?"

Chapter Eight

I jolted, spinning around to see who was behind me. Ash was frowning as he stared at me.

I clutched my chest. "You shouldn't do that to a girl who just found a dead body."

"Well, perhaps a girl shouldn't be snooping around the crime scene," he said.

"I wasn't snooping. I was just kind of . . . having a look to see if I found anything." I gestured over my shoulder.

"And what'd you find?" he asked.

Ash was clearly upset with me based on the tone of his voice and the frown on his face.

I pointed sheepishly toward the dumpster. "That thing on the ground there. It's a key fob for a Toyota. And this recipe card with the cherries on it."

"Why, thank you, Detective," he said, setting his hands on his hips. "I'll try to get some prints off of the key and see if there's a match for anyone who has a criminal record. But that doesn't really prove anything. And isn't that *your* recipe card?"

"Of course not," I said, sounding a bit too defensive for the circumstances.

He might be dismissing the clues I'd found, but *I* certainly wasn't going to rule them out. I wouldn't be catching any rides from strangers in Toyotas any time soon, that's all I was saying.

"Could you please not do this?" Ash asked.

"Do what?" I asked.

"Play Nancy Drew. I don't need a Jessica Fletcher out here either," he said.

I narrowed my eyes. "I'm not playing anyone. I'm just being Madeline Andersen."

"And being Madeline Andersen might get you into trouble," he said.

"Or out of trouble," I answered.

"All right, let's go somewhere else and talk." He pulled gently on my arm.

As Ash and I stepped out from behind the police tape at the end of the alley, the evening air was saturated with whispered accusations, questions, half truths, and secrets, suffocating us with its oppressive weight. People had already gathered on the sidewalk outside the alley, drawn by the police car lights. As Ash escorted me toward the front of my shop, the streetlights gave off a faint yellow glow, casting eerie shadows on the ground, and the off-key melody of the rain lulled us into an uneasy trance. I felt the hairs on the back of my neck standing up—an instinctive warning that something was massively wrong. He finally stopped in front of me and pinned me with a captivating stare. His voice was low, but it carried an unmistakable urgency.

"Tell me everything, Madeline," he said.

Without pause I recounted the whole story, from the first time Mallory came to my shop. I knew at times it probably seemed as if I was rambling, but I did that when I was nervous. His questions were sharp and incisive, probing and relentless. He wanted to know the details, the minutiae that only someone who had been there would be able to tell him. I struggled to answer each one, trying to recall things I hadn't even noticed before, especially about Grandma Ruth. Where exactly she had been standing when I came out of the bakery tonight, what she had been doing when I ran into her, and what she said. I answered him dutifully, but somehow I felt my replies weren't enough for him. He was really in detective mode.

He paused in what he was writing on his notepad and looked at me, as if he sensed my distress. "Listen," he said. "We'll find the truth, Madeline."

I couldn't bear looking in his eyes anymore, and I glanced up the street to see Thomas, arms crossed as he spoke to one of the other policemen. His shirt was rumpled and he looked disheveled. Made sense, what with his wife being dead. The fact he wasn't bawling his eyes out was impressive—or scary. I wasn't sure which. My eyes drifted to a figure beyond him—a man in a hoodie who was jotting something down on a notepad. One of the cops looked his way and gave him a nod. Maybe he was another detective I didn't know?

Ash's hand curved over my shoulder, and I turned back to face him.

"Let me know if you remember anything else," he said. His grip on my shoulder was firm yet comforting, like a promise that this ordeal would soon come to an end.

Ash sent me back inside the bakery with a police officer to accompany me as they continued to clear the scene. I was grateful to be leaving the alley. My head felt foggy and my body exhausted. I was anxious to get away so I could begin to process everything. Did the police suspect Grandma Ruth and me? After all, we had both publicly fought with Mallory only yesterday. Though I hardly thought an éclair would be considered a lethal weapon. Not to mention her being killed in the bakery's back alley of all places. Maybe she'd just slipped and hit her head and this was all a big misunderstanding.

After what felt like hours but was certainly quite less, Ash came inside the bakery and told me I could head home.

"If you're too shook up, one of us can drive you home," he said.

"My car is parked over there," I said, gesturing. "I'll be fine. I should go find Ruth so we can leave together, though."

Ash looked into my eyes briefly, apologetically, before saying, "You should go on ahead without her."

"Why would I do that?" My throat tightened with emotion.

"Ruth has been taken down to the station for further questioning."

"What? Why her but not me?"

"I can't really talk about it more, since this is an active investigation. I can say that it does appear that Mallory died from an act of violence. Your and your grandma's stories line up—Ruth left first and then you ran into her after hearing a noise. Which means she was alone in the alley and *she* was the first person to find Mallory's body."

"So?"

"So . . ." Ash trailed off and let my mind fill in the rest that he was unwilling or unable to provide.

They suspected Grandma Ruth had killed Mallory! It was unthinkable, but . . . they were operating from the circumstances, which I had to admit looked bad. I was stunned, too stunned to ask any more questions in the moment. My grandma, a murderer? I couldn't believe that anyone could think that would ever happen, no matter how violently she turned off the TV after the Raiders lost a game.

Ash and I walked silently to my car, the stars in the sky and the night air wrapping around us like a blanket. After saying goodbye, I sat in my car for a moment and called Grandma Ruth's phone, but it went straight to voicemail. I left a message urging her to call me as soon as she could and then I drove away. All the questions and chaos of the day seemed to be on a loop in my mind. I drove in an almost trance-like state, my car weaving back and forth as if it was being pulled along by a current.

As I turned off the main road and took the hairpin corner onto another small road, I noticed a pair of headlights in my rearview mirror that seemed to be mimicking my every move. My heart began to race, and my palms started to sweat. I gripped the steering wheel tighter. I wasn't sure who it was, but something didn't feel right. Was I being followed? No. There was no way—I was just on edge. A woman had died, and I was just anxious.

But the headlights followed me like hunting dogs, illuminating my every turn and heightening the panic in my chest. I felt their hungry gaze devouring me as I turned corner after corner, my anxiety mounting with each quickening second. But when I peeked over my shoulder, the headlights had vanished into the night, as if they were never there, and I shook my head at myself. It'd been hard to sleep lately, and even when I could, it was late nights and early mornings to keep the bakery well stocked and our customers happy. Sometimes when I was lying awake, trying to sleep, I'd think about my grandfather. If he'd be happy with what I'd done with the bakery. Rationally, I knew he would be. Of *course* he would be: all he ever cared about was other people's happiness. Grandma Ruth's, mine, his customers. He'd be happy to know that the bakery was still open; that it was still known to have some of the best pastries you could buy.

But knowing that didn't help me sleep. Nor did the meager profits the bakery was bringing in, or my own bank account that was looking a little lighter than usual after the costs of renovations. I found myself thinking about him now, about what he would be doing to help his wife who was stuck at the police station.

Insomnia-induced hallucination or not, I kept flicking my eyes to the rearview mirror, unsettled by the lingering sensation of being followed. This town all but shut down after dark, and the series of turns I'd taken didn't lead to any of the more populated areas of town. The little house I'd found to rent was in a fairly rural area, away from the kitsch of downtown. Someone making every turn I'd made was unusual enough that I decided I couldn't blame myself for wondering if they were following me, although it felt silly now that the car was gone.

In that moment, I felt grateful for the darkness of the night. It had masked my vulnerability and allowed me to keep driving without anyone knowing I was afraid. Thankfully the rest of the drive home was a short one. I pulled into the driveway and shut off the car. I sat there for several seconds. I had finally arrived at my destination, but I felt like I could barely move. My limbs were like lead weights, and my chest was so heavy with stress that it felt like I was carrying stones in my lungs. A body outside my floundering bakery. That was sure going to help sales. The weight of the stress had made me so exhausted I wasn't even sure I could walk to the front door.

I'd never been a very nervous person in LA. The size of the city had made me feel anonymous, sheltered by the constant presence of other people. I'd felt safe here too, among the windmills and tourists. But now, knowing there was a killer out there, and unsettled by my lack of sleep, the quiet town felt dangerous. Like I was totally alone, and nobody would hear me if I needed help. No matter how much I willed it, fear had crept into every fiber of my being. If someone had killed Mallory, then who was to say they wouldn't do it to me too? It was all too much. I wrapped my trembling hands around the cold brass doorknob as I listened for any sound that might give away an intruder lurking inside. Sweat built on my brow and the seconds felt like hours, stretching into eternity as I worked up the courage to just turn the knob. Taking one last deep breath, I braced myself for whatever awaited me on the other side of the door. I was just being paranoid, I reminded myself.

I yanked open the door and stepped inside, my eyes quickly taking stock of my surroundings with razor precision. Every inch of me was tense and ready, prepared to fight off any danger that might arise. But all I saw was the familiar setting of my home. Relief washed over me like a tidal wave. Of course I was safe.

Pepper came trotting out from the back of the house, having stayed home to snooze in a patch of sunlight all day. Some days he looked at me like I was crazy when I beckoned for him to come along to the bakery—and other days I don't think I could leave him home if I tried.

I crouched to scratch his head as he butted it up against me.

I took in the sights of my small home, with its smattering of well-worn furniture mostly borrowed from Grandma Ruth's larger house she was preparing to downsize from. My cozy living room, with my favorite armchair I shipped up from my LA apartment, seemed to invite me to sit and take a load off. The new book I had started yesterday lay on the end table, untouched today, its spine waiting to be cracked. But I couldn't find solace in its pages today; my mind was too full of thoughts and heavy with worry.

I trudged my way toward the kitchen, hoping to find some kind of distraction, or perhaps just a glass of cold water, before I went upstairs to my bedroom. I needed something that would help me escape the world. Just until I could make it to safety behind the doors of my bedroom. I couldn't wait to be tucked safely under the covers, hiding from the world and catching a few moments of peace before I returned to my obligations. But even then, would I be able to find any peace?

Chapter Nine

The next morning, my anxiety was still running high as I stepped out my front door. After leaving multiple voicemails and sending numerous texts, late in the night I finally received a short text back from Grandma Ruth. She said she was back home and would see me in the morning. I had decided to bring Pepper with me in his carrier, as I figured we could both use his comforting presence at work. He seemed unimpressed with the warm day, as usual. The gray sky was just beginning to lighten, and I hoped that would also help ease the dread inside me. Even if just a little bit. Raindrops had been falling from the heavens above all morning. It reminded me of a watercolor painting my parents had on their living room wall where all the colors melted together into a warm mess. A mess—that was how I felt right now.

I had decided to park my car some distance from the shop and walk the rest of the way to work for exercise since the sun was rising earlier in the day now. It was a therapeutic stroll that allowed me to take in the fresh air and enjoy my surroundings. Pepper was meowing his displeasure at being in the carrier I held in my arms. As I walked down the sidewalk,

I passed by freshly mowed lawns and colorful flower beds that lined the streets. The air was still a little cool, but the sun was beginning to warm the morning breeze. I navigated around the puddles on the sidewalk as I hurried toward the bakery.

I couldn't help but keep my head on a swivel, and my eyes caught on a group across the street. Among them was Frankie, and I cringed, instantly worried he might try to talk to me again—I'd never been that good with teens—but he only smiled briefly before ducking into a car with the rest of the gaggle of boys he was with, their laughter and chatter filling the air. It was nice to see him hanging out with friends his own age, just having fun, unbothered by the very adult problems I had been enmeshed in. Maybe they'd find him an age-appropriate girl to crush on.

As I stood on the sidewalk, the morning sun casting a warm glow around me, I noticed Mrs. Castille across the sidewalk too. She was waving goodbye to Frankie, but he didn't notice her. Then she looked over at me and waved, and I took it as a sign, a perfect opportunity to nip the whole thing in the bud, just like Grandma Ruth said I should.

"Hey, Mrs. Castille," I called out as I crossed the street to where she was standing. "I hope I'm not bothering you."

She smiled warmly, shaking her head. "Not at all, Madeline. I was just seeing Frankie off before I run some errands in town."

I hesitated for a moment, unsure how to broach the subject delicately. Finally, I took a deep breath and plunged ahead. "I wanted to talk to you about Frankie," I began, my words tumbling out in a rush. "I thought . . . Well, I think he might have had a little crush on me. I feel silly for even mentioning it, but it's just a little awkward."

She listened attentively, her expression thoughtful. "Oh, Madeline," she said gently, placing a comforting hand on my arm. "Don't feel silly. Kids can be tricky to read sometimes. But I'm sure Frankie just admires you. His dad's a business owner too."

I offered her a small smile. "I appreciate it. Maybe if he's interested in helping out, we could find some work for him to do around the bakery. And I'm sorry for bothering you so early."

She waved off my apology with a dismissive gesture. "No bother at all, Madeline. And that's kind of you to think of him. He might like that; I'll mention it to him. Anytime you need to talk, I'm here."

"Stop by the bakery anytime," I said with a wave and continued on my way, feeling a weight lifted from my shoulders. Perhaps things weren't as complicated with Frankie as I'd feared after all.

I wasn't looking forward to walking by Mrs. Johnson's house. According to Grandma Ruth, Mrs. Johnson was the town gossip, and I suspected that she'd confront me about the murder and dig for any details I might have. I sped up my pace as I passed by Mrs. Johnson's house. Sure enough, I spotted her sitting on her front porch swing, eagerly awaiting my approach. She stood up and ambled over to the steps, her eyes narrowing as she sized me up, stopping me in my tracks.

I knew I hadn't done anything wrong, but the look on her face said otherwise. She stood before me, hands on her hips, an expression of disappointment and disapproval on her face. I could see the silver streaks in her dark gray hair, pulled back into a tight twist that matched her personality. Immediately, a low hiss filled the air as Pepper declared his displeasure.

I held on tightly to the carrier, feeling like my cat was trying to protect me from Mrs. Johnson's accusatory gaze.

"Good morning, Mrs. Johnson," I said hesitantly.

"Well, if it isn't the little missy who knows all about the dead body at her bakery," she said with a devious glint in her eye.

I suppressed a sigh and tried to maintain a neutral expression.

"And what do you have to say for yourself?" she asked.

I took a deep breath and explained that I had nothing to do with the murder. "It just happened to be near my bakery."

"That Ruth," Mrs. Johnson said, sniffing haughtily. "I heard she got in quite the scuffle with that poor dead woman."

My cheeks went hot. "I don't know what you're implying, Mrs. Johnson."

I felt as if I was already in court in front of a judge. Mrs. Johnson didn't seem to be satisfied with my answer, but she waved me off with a warning to "keep my nose out of other people's business."

I wondered how accidentally finding a murder victim was putting my nose in other people's business. But I was just thankful she wasn't bombarding me with more questions. Even before I reached the alleyway behind my shop, I felt a sense of dread in the air. The crime scene awaited me at the bakery. There was no getting away from that. I debated even looking at the newspaper. I knew Mallory's murder would be front page news.

Fear coursed through me as I shuffled my feet down the sidewalk. I thought of Mallory, her lifeless body slumped over in a pool of her own blood. I hadn't been able to rest all night, flashbacks of the scene stuck in my mind. Not only was I worried about Grandma Ruth and whether customers would return to my bakery but also if the murderer still lurked nearby. Who had done this to Mallory? Thoughts spun wildly in my mind as I tried to think of people who might be suspects. She'd certainly made a lot of enemies in town in a short amount of time.

As I neared the bakery, I passed by the local bookstore and noticed the morning paper in the window. I couldn't believe my eyes. There, on the front page of the *Solvang Gazette*, were two pictures side-by-side. One was of Grandma Ruth from one of the school yearbooks, with her jersey on and whistle around her neck. The other picture was of me, arms crossed, looking directly into the camera with a determined expression, below the headline: "Local Woman Finds Murder Victim!" It was a picture of me from a press release the LA restaurant had put out when they first hired me as the pâtissier, and I winced at the glare in my eyes. I'd been so afraid that I wasn't ready for such a high-profile position, and the defensiveness was all over my face.

Of course I had to dash inside the bookstore and buy a copy of the paper. After quickly reading the article, I was stunned. The article went on to describe Grandma Ruth's discovery of Mallory's body in great detail, alongside a recap of the theatrics at the bakeoff. I couldn't help but panic a little. I finished reading and shoved the newspaper into my bag. It wasn't exactly something I'd want to add to my scrapbook.

When I arrived at the shop, I discovered that the police were there again—or still there, I wasn't sure which. Why was I surprised? No doubt they wanted to look for anything they might have missed the night before. The alley was filled with the smell of coffee, along with the sharp, salty scent of blood—an odd and unpleasant mixture. I tried to take it all in, but my mind was too focused on what would happen next. Would Ash find the killer and clear Grandma Ruth's name? I took one last deep breath, regretting it after inhaling the strange scent once more, and then stepped into the shop.

I tried to put the crime scene out of my mind as I entered the bakery kitchen. It had been a long night, filled with shock and questions, but I knew I had work to do. I had to forget about my many questions and focus instead on the task of baking fresh croissants and éclairs for the day. It was nice to be in a small town sometimes—if I had a bad night's sleep back in LA, I couldn't have just shown up a few hours late for work. Here, starting late was par for the course. Most of the small businesses kept casual hours, leaving handwritten notes in the door that said things like "we're at lunch, be back later!"

I placed Pepper's carrier on the ground and released him. He dashed off to his bed in the corner, grateful to be freed.

There was no sign of Grandma Ruth yet so I got started to help distract myself. My hands trembled as I prepped the ingredients, the usually familiar motions of my routine taking their time to come to me today. I worked quickly and efficiently, trying to ignore the lingering heaviness in my chest. When I had finished prepping the dough, I put the baking trays into the oven and wiped the sweat from my forehead. With any luck, I would still have customers despite the crime scene outside, and the aroma of freshly baked pastries filling the bakery would be more than enough of a distraction from the events of last night. I looked out the window into the empty street and said a silent prayer.

My breath hitched in my throat as the kitchen door suddenly rattled.

"Oh, it's just you," I said, relieved.

"Did you think the boogeyman had come for you?" Grandma Ruth asked as she placed her big pocketbook down on the counter.

"I thought maybe the killer was coming after me," I said.

"I'll say. I hardly slept a wink last night," she said.

I nodded and attempted a smile. "It's hard not to worry."

"Ash will solve the case soon and we can put this fear behind us," she said, but her words lacked confidence.

"I guess," I said, letting the unspoken questions hang in the air.

"I can only stay for an hour," Grandma Ruth said.

"Wait—why?"

"I've been asked to go down to the police station to answer a few more questions," Grandma Ruth explained.

"What more could they possibly want to ask you after keeping you there all night? You just threw out a bag of garbage!" I paused took a deep breath. They were wasting precious time, talking to Grandma Ruth again when there was a real killer out there somewhere. Grandma Ruth stared warily at me as I grabbed my bag.

"Don't get any ideas," she said. "They're going to figure this out, and things will get back to normal."

"I just need fresh air. I'm going for a walk. Just take the trays out of the oven when the timer rings."

Grandma Ruth raised an eyebrow. "Now, don't try and get involved any further into this mess. Ash knows I didn't hurt that woman. They'll just ask me a few more questions, and I'll be back in time for lunch."

I just waved and headed out the door, careful to avoid making any promises. It was already too late to take her advice. A sense of unease hung heavily around me as I walked down the sidewalk. The discovery of a victim behind my shop in such a short time span had rattled me to the core. It wasn't just the grisly scene that had me on edge but the scrutiny and suspicion on Grandma Ruth that followed. I knew the whispers around town would only grow louder, and the newspaper hadn't been kind either. Accusatory glances from the townspeople I passed, along with the police's questions the night before, made me feel guilty of something rather than a victim of circumstance. Murder—or rather, a murder victim—had literally come knocking at my bakery's door, and I was caught in the crossfire.

I knew I needed to take matters into my own hands. I probably couldn't actually solve a murder case, but I could do something, find some evidence that would help the police, or find a way to turn the tide of public opinion to protect Grandma Ruth's reputation until the truth came out. I only knew that something needed to be done quickly, to alleviate the cloud of fear and unease hanging over Grandma Ruth. Not to mention protecting our business. As evidenced by their interest in Grandma Ruth as a suspect, the police might spin in circles for weeks, unable to find concrete leads. The cloud of suspicion might never lift from over our heads—and our bakery. The last thing I wanted was for my beloved grandma to be threatened. Or the bakery that she and my grandpa had worked for years to build and that was now the heart of our livelihood, to become a scene of fear and suspicion.

To start, I needed to piece together the events leading up to the tragedy, combing through my memory for any hint of unusual occurrences or suspicious figures in the days prior. The need to exonerate Grandma Ruth made me want to scrutinize every detail, follow every lead, and talk to anyone who might have even the merest hint of what had truly happened. I wasn't just seeking justice for the victim; I was fighting to protect Grandma Ruth and save our life's work.

Chapter Ten

When I got back from my walk, a few customers had gathered outside the bakery doors, waiting for us to open. That was a bit unusual—I suspected they were hungry for information about the night before more than fresh pastries. But a customer is a customer, so I unlocked the doors and let them in. Unlike her normally boisterous self, Grandma Ruth opted to remain back in the kitchen, away from prying eyes and unwanted questions. I certainly couldn't blame her.

Among the locals who trickled into the bakery was Suzette Abbott. Suzette was an occasional customer, but I'd never found her waiting outside the doors before opening. But she'd always been friendly with me, and I had appreciated how she and the other judges of the baking contest had stood up for me after Mallory's wild accusations. Suzette lingered near the counter, as if waiting for me to strike up a conversation. So I decided to take the bait.

"Bonjour, Suzette. What can I help you with this morning?"

"Well, I'm not sure . . ." she said, scanning the interior of the bakery display. It felt like she was stalling for time.

I decided to push things along. "You probably heard about what happened here last night. Or read about it in the paper."

"As a matter of fact, I did! How horrible! How are you and Ruth holding up? Is she here?"

"She's here, but she's working in the back. We had a long night."

"I can only imagine! That poor woman! You know, I was the one who sold her and husband their house. They only moved here weeks ago and now . . . it's too terrible to think about."

At the mention of Mallory's husband, my mind flashed back to the sight of him in the alley the night before, and then to the one other time I'd seen him, when he came to fetch Mallory from the bakery after her phone-related freakout.

"What's her husband's name again?" I asked Suzette.

"Thomas. He always seemed much less excitable than Mallory, if you know what I mean. He did most of the business related to the sale, all of the paperwork and such. Which I guess makes sense since he works for that car manufacturer outside of town. I think he's pretty high up the executive food chain there. That's why they moved out here in the first place; he got promoted and transferred. Mallory didn't seem particularly thrilled about it."

Suzette was proving a wealth of information with very little prodding on my part. I simply nodded and let her keep talking.

"You know," Suzette said, lowering her voice and leaning over the counter toward me. A couple of the other locals nearby craned their necks to try and catch what we were saying. "I heard something else. That Thomas had just taken out a quite sizeable new life insurance policy on Mallory. He did it at the same time as the insurance for the new house. I had to answer some questions with the insurer relating to the sale. And you also know what they always say, about the spouse being the first and best suspect . . ."

My mind swirled with all of this new insight into Mallory and Thomas. It certainly gave me a jumping-off point in terms of redirecting the police's attention away from Grandma Ruth—and toward Thomas. I needed some time to process it all and figure out my next steps.

"Well, I'd better tend to the other customers," I said, trying to remain polite but also steer Suzette on her way. "How about some éclairs, since you enjoyed them so much the other day at the contest? You did come here for some breakfast, right?"

"Oh, right! Yes, éclairs would hit the spot. Some of these café crème ones would be perfect, along with a coffee to go. Three sugars."

As I assembled Suzette's order and then turned my attention to the remaining customers, I decided I was going to start my investigation with Mallory's husband, Thomas. After the initial rush, the bakery emptied out. The locals mostly seemed disappointed by my brief, noncommittal answers to their leading questions about Mallory's murder so they didn't linger. Soon it was time for Grandma Ruth to depart for her second round at the police station. After exchanging what I hoped were encouraging words, I saw her off—I noticed she left through the front doors and not the back way through the alley, which was still marked off with police caution tape.

Left alone in the bakery with a bunch of unwanted thoughts, I took action. I made a call to the car manufacturer that Suzette had mentioned, the largest outside of town. I certainly didn't expect Thomas to be at work the morning after his wife had been murdered, but I figured I could speak with one of his coworkers or even his supervisor and glean some additional information. I was therefore very surprised when the receptionist told me that Mr. Gates was in the office. That itself seemed wildly suspicious to me—shouldn't he at home, grieving? Or at the police station like Grandma Ruth, answering questions? What could he possibly be doing at work so soon after his wife's tragic and sudden death? Checking up on the insurance policy that Suzette had mentioned, maybe? I thanked the receptionist and quickly ended the call so I could process my many new questions.

Given how slow business was, I made a quick decision. I flipped the sign on the bakery door to *Be Back Soon!*, checked that Pepper's water bowl was full, and then headed out. I was going to Thomas's office. I googled the name of the company and made the short drive to their office building. Once inside, the grand, modern lobby stretched out before me. The walls were adorned with sleek artwork, and a crystal chandelier hung from the high ceiling. People in business attire moved purposefully, engrossed in their own tasks and not paying attention to me. Which served me well, as I wanted to slip in under the radar.

I marched into the lobby with determination. I'd never had a good poker face, but I figured if I acted as if I had an appointment with Thomas that they had somehow forgotten about I might be able to guilt my way into seeing him. I wasn't sure if he'd remember seeing me at the bakery earlier and again at the bakeoff or had been too distracted by Mallory's behavior to have even noticed. But either way, once I was in his office I'd have the opportunity to question him. I clutched a folder tightly under my arm. I'd grabbed it from the backseat of my car. I hoped that would help me look like I was on an official business matter. It only contained my scribbled notes, but no one needed to know that.

My steps echoed against the polished marble floor as I headed toward the reception desk. The young, dark-haired receptionist, presumably the same one I'd spoken to on the phone earlier, smiled at me warmly as she sat behind a pristine desk.

"Good morning. How may I assist you?" she asked cheerfully.

"I have an appointment with Mr. Gates," I said. I realized I didn't know the exact time and couldn't check my watch so I improvised. Badly. "For, uh . . . now."

"I'm sorry, ma'am, but Mr. Gates is in a meeting at the moment. And I don't see any other appointments on his schedule. Can I ask who you are and what this is regarding?"

"I'm . . . Lisa Markham. I'm a client. We made the appointment weeks ago."

The name had just popped into my head. Making things up like this in the moment was something of an adrenaline rush.

"I'm so sorry, Ms. Markham, but I'm still not seeing anything. It would be best if I notify Mr. Gates about your visit and set up an appointment for a later time. His time is valuable, and we need to respect the proper channels."

It looked as if she wasn't going to make this easy for me.

"But I came all the way from LA for this meeting! Can I please just see him for a few minutes?"

"Let me see what I can do. Please take a seat, and I'll inform you as soon as there's an available slot in Mr. Gates's schedule."

I thanked her, walked over to a plush leather sofa nearby and sat down. The receptionist dialed a number on her phone and spoke quietly into it. Then it hit me. What if she called security instead? I supposed that was a chance I'd have to take.

As my eyes took in the opulent surroundings, my mind was consumed with thoughts of imminent confrontation. The lobby bustled with activity as employees passed by, exchanging nods and brief greetings. I watched the buzz of activity swirl around me and listened to the chattering voices that filled the air. Time seemed to stretch on for far too long as I impatiently waited. As I waited, I opened the folder that I'd brought, reviewing the evidence I'd gathered so far. Which really wasn't much. Reading over my hastily scribbled notes, my determination intensified. With so little to go on, I really needed to confront Thomas Gates. And hold him accountable for his actions—if he had killed his wife.

The receptionist abruptly motioned for me from behind her desk. My stomach tensed with dread at every step.

"Mr. Gates will see you now," she said icily. "Go down the hallway to your right."

I didn't linger, and, after a quick thank you, I headed to the office. I made my way down the long hallway in silence, passing a few other employees on my way. I finally reached the end of the hallway and stopped in front of a large wooden door with "Thomas Gates" on a nameplate on the wall next to it. As I grasped the cold metal office doorknob I felt a rush of energy surge through me. With a loud creak, the door opened, swinging open more than I'd anticipated. I lunged forward in an attempt to catch the door, but the momentum was too strong and it slammed into the wall with a thunderous boom, shaking the entire room. From his desk, Thomas Gates stared at me with a frown.

"Sorry about that," I said as I closed the door as gently as possible behind me.

This hadn't gotten off to a good start. Thomas sat behind a big mahogany desk. His dark eyes were hard to read. At the least, he didn't seem overly distraught for a man whose wife had been murdered just the night before. And I liked to think I was a good judge of character. His hands were clenched tightly together as he waited for me to speak. I had a line of questioning I intended to get out, and I didn't want anything to get in my way of finding the answers.

Every nerve in my body was on high alert from the knowledge that I could be alone in a room with a killer. Either that or I was about to confront a grieving widower and accuse him of being a killer. I had one goal: to uncover the truth behind his wife's murder, so I couldn't let him intimidate me. Moving slowly, I pulled out the chair across from his desk and settled gently onto the seat. I studied him carefully. My nerves were high as I tapped my fingers against the armrest of the leather chair.

I tried to act the part, keeping my face composed, but I had no idea what my plan really was. Thomas was a middle-aged man. He wore an expensive-looking sky-blue tailored suit. He was about what I'd imagined but more put together than I'd expect a man whose wife was murdered yesterday would be. He looked me up and down from his spot behind his desk. He seemed somewhat surprised yet composed. If he recognized me from our brief encounter days earlier at the bakery, it didn't register on his face.

"Mr. Gates, we need to talk," I said, trying to sound confident. I pushed my shoulders back and held my head higher. Inside though I felt like a scared little mouse. Just like La Petite Souris, the little mouse in one of my favorite French fairy tales.

"Who are you and what do you want?" he asked with a frown.

I was relieved that he apparently didn't recognize me. "Mr. Gates," I said, my voice strong and even. "I'm here to ask you some questions about your wife's death."

So much for being subtle. I hadn't planned on just blurting that out.

"Again, who are you?" he asked, looking me up and down again.

I debated telling the truth or continuing to spin a story. I went with the latter. "I'm a private investigator."

"And who hired you?" he asked with a frown.

I took a deep breath before answering his question, trying to buy some time to think of how I should answer him. He'd asked a good question, and I wasn't sure what to say. A knot twisted in my stomach as I considered my options. I cleared my throat nervously and thought carefully before responding. Drawing on every ounce of my acting abilities, I gave him a tight-lipped smile and said, "Actually, there was another murder case that was similar to your wife's and I'm looking into that. I want to find out if there's a connection."

It must have been a good answer, because his expression eased and his tense posture relaxed somewhat. I couldn't believe I'd come up with that response.

He stared at me for a moment before finally speaking. "What do you want to know? I've already spoken to the police for hours." He sounded weary and a bit irritated.

I took a deep breath before beginning my questions, determined not to let him intimidate me in this room where he likely felt so powerful. One by one, I asked him each of my questions, all while carefully watching his facial expressions for any sign of guilt or deception. I began with indirect inquiries, which was something I'd watched on episodes of *CSI*.

"How would you describe your relationship with your wife?" I asked.

"We had a great relationship. Married for twenty years."

I had a feeling he would answer that way. Of course he wouldn't say their relationship was bad, but I looked for any signs of deception. I glanced around the room to look for anything out of the ordinary. I only saw the typical things you'd see in an office like a filing cabinet and papers covering his desk. On the floor nearby was an overnight bag. It was unzipped and I spotted what looked like jeans and a white T-shirt inside. Was he planning a trip?

"Did you notice any changes in your wife's behavior or mood before her death?" I knew she'd acted a bit unhinged at my shop, but would he tell me more?

"Mallory was passionate about the things she believed in," he answered.

I shifted gears. "Can you tell me about your whereabouts during the time your wife was killed?"

His voice hardened like steel as he spat out the words, "This feels more like you're accusing me. Are you questioning my integrity?" His eyes narrowed and his jaw clenched with rising anger.

"Just standard questions," I said. I shifted in my seat. How could I get him to answer the question? "It would help me a lot if you answered. And maybe I'll be able to find the person who killed your wife."

He sighed and then said, "I was working late last night and had an important meeting scheduled when she was killed. I have colleagues who can confirm my whereabouts. I met the police at the crime scene once I was notified."

It seemed like he had thought out that answer and was quick to offer an alibi. I suppose Ash had already asked him that same question. I wondered what Ash thought of the answer and if he'd confirmed it already with Thomas's colleagues.

"Is there anything you'd like to share about your relationship that might help me understand what happened to your wife?"

"How the hell am I supposed to know? I don't know who killed her." His voice quivered with barely contained fury. He'd spat out each word like venom, his face contorting into a mask of guilt. The air around him vibrated with electric tension, crackling with a raw intensity that made it clear something wasn't right.

He was being awfully defensive. Was that because he had something to hide? Regardless, I clearly needed to change directions in order to keep the conversation going. "I know losing someone you loved for so many years is incredibly difficult," I softly uttered.

He nodded but didn't respond.

"How are you coping with your wife's passing?" I asked.

His eyes searched mine as he spoke. "It's been hard," he finally said.

I watched him closely, scrutinizing his every movement. Was he being sincere or was this all an act? I couldn't tell. He stood and walked over to the window. He stood there for a few moments, his gaze lost on the distant horizon.

"I'm still trying to figure it out," he murmured, more to himself than to me. "I feel like I should be grieving more, like I should feel the pain of her loss more deeply. But I just can't seem to bring myself to do it." He sighed heavily and turned back to me. "I guess I'm still in shock," he said. "Most people would think it's crazy to be back at work so soon, but I just sort of found myself falling into my normal routine. Maybe work is a good distraction? I don't know."

"Well, sometimes people make mistakes and find themselves in situations they never intended. Is there anything you need to get off your chest?" I asked. Every muscle in my body was tensed up with worry of what would come next.

"Do you think that I had something to do with my wife's murder? That's crazy. How dare you suggest such a thing? There's nothing more I want to say," he said.

The room filled with a heavy silence. We were like two chess opponents stuck in a standstill, unable to make their next move until the other did.

Finally, I broke the silence. "Tell me what happened last night," I said. "Did you talk to her?" My voice was low, yet there was an unmistakable edge of steel to my words.

"I already told the police. Mallory called me before my meeting and said she was going to town, but she didn't say why. She asked me to pick her up later."

I studied Thomas intently as he sat across from me, his expression a mixture of defiance and uncertainty. The conversation had been going on for a while, and I sensed his restlessness. He no doubt wanted me to leave. Maybe after I left and I had time to reflect back on this conversation I'd notice any discrepancies in his account. Was he doing nothing more than weaving a complex web of lies and misdirection? If so, then I was determined to unravel it.

"So, you're saying that you left the meeting around ten o'clock?" I asked.

Thomas hesitated, as though debating whether to tell the truth. "Yes," he finally said. "I left around ten."

I raised an eyebrow, not entirely convinced. "But according to the security footage, you left at nine. That leaves a whole hour unaccounted for."

I had no idea if that was true. But I'd seen this trick on TV too.

Thomas shifted uncomfortably in his seat and cleared his throat. "Well, I . . . I might have left a bit earlier than I initially thought. Wait. I remember now. I left at fifteen after nine."

That was still forty-five minutes earlier than he'd just claimed. Had he just incriminated himself? I nodded, my suspicions deepening. I began to think more and more that Thomas was the culprit. His story was becoming increasingly difficult to believe, and I wondered if I'd be able to build a case against him. I just needed evidence to prove it.

"You asked me a question, and I gave you an answer," he said with a strange sense of calm. "Are we done here?"

"Look, Mr. Gates, if there's anything else, anything at all that you'd like to share with me, now is the time. I'm just trying to solve a crime and would like to rule out any connection you might have to your wife's murder. You know, the truth can be liberating. Holding on to secrets can take a toll on a person."

"We are done talking, Ms. Markham." He stood up from his desk and crossed his arms over his chest with an air of satisfaction that made me uneasy.

He seemed pleased at how well he'd handled himself during our conversation. But I suspected there was much more than just self-satisfaction hiding beneath that exterior. My breath quickened as he walked around his desk and stood directly beside me. I could feel his presence looming over me.

"I didn't mean to upset you," I said.

"That will be all," he said dismissively, giving me one final look before turning fully away from me to face the window behind his desk once more.

I left without having acquired any hard proof that Thomas Gates killed his wife—but I was going to keep my eye on him. Maybe I just hadn't asked the right question yet.

Chapter Eleven

I made it back to the bakery just in time to reopen before Grandma Ruth returned. She didn't seem very eager to discuss the latest round of questioning, other than it was a lot of repetitive queries about how and when she'd found Mallory's body. I didn't press her, given that she'd just undergone hours of interrogation. I figured work would be a good distraction for us both. An order of croissants had to be filled within the hour and so we immediately got to work. But after only a few minutes, the bell over the bakery door jingled. I looked up from the dough I was kneading. My hands froze when I saw Natalie standing there, shifting nervously from one foot to the other. The last time I'd seen her, at the baking contest, she had been angry and accusatory. Now she looked . . . hesitant. Apologetic, even.

"Madeline," she started, her voice softer than I'd ever heard it. "Can we talk for a second?"

I was unsure whether to smile and talk or tell her I was too busy. After everything that had gone down at the baking contest, she was the last person I'd expected to walk in. She'd accused me of sabotage, of playing dirty to win. The way she'd looked at me—like I was beneath her, like she was certain I'd done it—still stung.

"I'm kind of busy," I said, nodding toward the dough on the counter. "Unless you're here to order something."

Natalie winced, brushing her hair back from her face. "I'm not. I—I just needed to say that I'm sorry. I made a mistake."

That got my attention. I wiped my hands on my apron, then leaned against the counter. "What kind of mistake?"

She bit her lip and looked around the bakery, as if stalling. Finally, she met my gaze. "I found out it wasn't you who stole my ingredients at the contest."

"Oh," I said, sighing the word with relief. This town was too small to have any enemies. "Who was it?"

Natalie hesitated, then exhaled like the confession had been bottled up too long. "It was Mallory. She let it slip that she had taken the ingredients. Before she . . . died."

My stomach flipped. Mallory. Of course it was Mallory. She'd been beyond angry that she hadn't won.

Natalie must've noticed my expression because she quickly added, "I shouldn't have jumped to conclusions. I was wrong to accuse you, Madeline. I let my insecurities get in the way, and I'm sorry."

Her apology hung in the air between us, sincere but awkward. I didn't know what to say. Part of me wanted to shove it back in her face, to remind her how awful she'd been. But another part of me—probably the one that believed in second chances—knew holding a grudge wouldn't solve anything.

I let out a slow breath, meeting her eyes. "It really hurt, you know. You didn't even give me a chance to defend myself."

Natalie nodded quickly. "I know. And I regret that. I was just so . . . so angry. And Mallory had this way of stirring up things."

"Yes, she certainly did," I muttered, shaking my head.

A hint of a smile touched Natalie's lips.

I sighed, uncrossing my arms. "Look, I appreciate the apology. I really do. But this isn't just about you and me. What Mallory did isn't right, and it's not fair to anyone else in that competition. But she's gone now. I think there's more important things to be worried about now than a baking competition."

Natalie's face hardened. "You know, if there's one thing I hate more than being wrong, it's being played."

"Well, hopefully you can believe me now when I say I'm not the type to break the rules to win," I said. The tension between us seemed to ease. Natalie glanced around the bakery again, then back at me. "So . . . do you think we can move past this?"

I studied her for a moment before nodding. "Yeah, I think we can. But don't expect me to go easy on you at the next baking contest."

Natalie grinned, a glimmer of her old competitiveness shining through. "I wouldn't dream of it."

As she left, the bakery felt a little lighter, but I knew a storm was still brewing in town.

After lunch, Grandma Ruth convinced me to take a break, thinking I'd been hard at work at the bakery all during her absence. I agreed to lock up the bakery for a bit as we still had hardly any customers anyway. Everyone walking by was just peeking down the alley next door, not coming inside for anything.

Grandma Ruth still refused to tell me anything more about her second trip to the station; she just insisted everything would be fine. I knew she was just trying to dissuade me from getting further involved. But I had my own secrets to keep: never, ever mentioning my visit to Thomas.

We dropped Pepper off at home to enjoy the air conditioning. The midday heat clung heavily in the air as we left the bakery, and I felt like I was suffocating. Grandma Ruth was clearly exhausted after her back-to-back stints at the police station, so I convinced her to head home for a nap while I went back to the bakery. It didn't require all that much convincing; she conceded rather quickly. Once I reopened, customers drifted in and out, mostly tourists with some locals and regulars mixed in. I was especially grateful for the tourists, since they were seemingly unaware of Mallory's murder and therefore didn't ask any pesky questions. Thankfully, if any of them had noticed the police caution tape blocking off the alley next door, it hadn't deterred them from stopping inside the bakery.

After about a half hour with no customers, the bell above the front door dinged, indicating a new arrival. Ash strode inside, looking rather serious.

"Do you have news?" I asked, forgetting to even say hello amid my concern for Grandma Ruth and her precarious situation.

"Not really," he admitted. "I mostly came by to see how the two of you are faring."

"Grandma Ruth was understandably worn out so she went home early to rest. As for me . . . I guess I'm doing as okay as can be under the circumstances. There's no one else here right now—why don't we sit down and take a coffee break?"

Ash plopped down on one of the nearby wrought-iron chairs while I brought over a plate of spandauers and two cups of coffee.

"This hasn't been easy on her, to say the least . . . and now this. You know she's innocent, Ash," I said, sliding one of the cups across the table toward him.

He hesitated, not meeting my eyes.

"What? What is it? Did something else happen?"

"I really shouldn't say," he said. "But it will probably be in the paper or at least will be spread around town in no time. We took your grandma's shoes into evidence, the ones she was wearing last night. And there's blood on them. Mallory's blood."

My own blood chilled at his words, but it didn't stop me from rushing to Grandma Ruth's defense. "She was standing right by Mallory—the alley was so dark, she may have even stepped on her before she realized what was happening. So of course there might be some blood on her shoes. That doesn't mean she killed her. She's not capable of that!"

"You and I may know that from experience, but the evidence is mounting. She had motive thanks to their very public arguments and Mallory's vendetta against you and this place. She essentially assaulted Mallory at the baking contest. Mallory would have been within her rights to press charges, even it was just an éclair that got thrown. And Grandma Ruth had the time and means to commit the act before you discovered her."

"This is ridiculous! By that logic, I should be a suspect as well. I had just as much of a grudge against Mallory."

"We're not ruling out anything. But people are always eager to find an answer quickly in situations like this, and often the most obvious one is the easiest and fastest solution."

"Even if it's the wrong one?" I cried indignantly. I considered telling him what I had learned earlier about Thomas and the insurance policy, but I wanted to gather stronger evidence before presenting it to him. Plus I absolutely did not want him to know I was poking around, based on our conversation in the alley the night before.

Ash didn't answer my question, just picked up one of the spandauers and admired it for a moment. Then he said, "Back in the day, your grandpa would bring a tray of these after every one of our games, win or lose. I always remember how proud he looked off on the sidelines, watching Ruth lead us to victory." He took a bite and after another moment said, "You know, this tastes exactly like I remember way back in high school."

"I'm using my grandpa's recipe. This is my family we're talking about, Ash. They are good people."

"I know. I've known your grandma since I was a teen."

"My grandma mentioned that you were rather wild back in the day," I said, happy to change the subject to something lighter. But I also figured it couldn't hurt to further remind Ash about his history with Grandma Ruth.

Ash chuckled. "I don't know about 'wild,' but I definitely was adventurous as a teen. Your grandma was good at keeping all of the players in line, though. We were way more scared of her than the head coach, even though he was this big burly dude."

"I can believe that. Did you leave Solvang after high school?"

"I did, for a while. I traveled; I went to college. But I ended up right back here. There's something special about this place, for all its quirks. It's unique. And the people who live and work here all year round, not just the tourists that come for the day, really want to be here. They want to make it better. At least I do."

"That's admirable. I liked the pace and variety of LA, but it did feel ephemeral at times. People would move in and move out before you knew it. I felt like I was always looking for a new friend to replace one who got a job somewhere else and moved on. Not to mention dating . . ." Slightly embarrassed, I trailed off.

"What about dating?" Ash asked neutrally, turning his cup slightly on the table. Avoiding eye contact. I squinted. Maybe it was just polite conversation.

"It wasn't easy, let's just put it that way."

"It's not all that easy here either," he confessed, his eyes lifting back to mine. I was finding it easier to talk to him now that my mind was on something else like murder. "Small town, smaller dating pool. And everyone knows everyone else's business."

"That part I've learned for myself, quickly." We lapsed into an awkward silence. Since I had him cornered, though, I had to take advantage of the situation and ask some more questions about the case. My curiosity about the ongoing investigation burned inside me.

"Has there been any other progress with the investigation Any other clues?" I asked, trying to sound casual but feeling my pulse quicken with anticipation.

Ash hesitated and took a drink. "It's complicated. Still looking into all the leads," he replied vaguely.

I sensed the distance in his response. "I know it's a tough case," I offered, trying not to push too hard. "But you know, if you ever need an extra pair of eyes or something . . ."

"I already warned you, Madeline, don't get involved any more than you already are. As you can see this is dangerous. You're not starring in your very own episode of *Murder, She Wrote.*"

"I'm more of a *Great British Bake Off* fan," I quipped.

He frowned. "You know what I mean." Ash drained what was left in his coffee cup. "I should get back to work." But his gaze lingered on me.

"Thanks for checking in," I said, feeling a mix of gratitude and disappointment that our conversation hadn't breached deeper waters.

Ash met my eyes, a flicker of something unspoken passing between us. "Stay safe, Madeline. Please."

Chapter Twelve

The next day while closing up, despite the cozy warmth of the bakery, a shiver raced up my spine. It was like an electric current that pulsed through every nerve in my body, making the hairs on my arms stand up. As I looked around, searching for the source of my unease, I saw no one. But still, it felt as if someone was watching me. Perhaps it was merely a figment of my imagination brought on by the eerie quietness of the alleyway.

Or maybe . . . just maybe it was something more sinister than that. *No, don't let your imagination get the best of you*, I reminded myself. I'd always had a way of letting my mind think of worst-case scenarios. Maybe I watched too much crime TV. Whatever it was, I quickened my pace and hurried toward my car. I'd had to park a good distance away from the bakery that morning because the alley was still roped off with crime scene tape.

As I walked, it felt like someone was following me. I kept glancing over my shoulder, but I didn't see anyone directly behind me. Nevertheless, I quickened my pace.

When I turned the corner onto a narrow side street, I saw him. A tall, lanky man, walking a few paces behind me. He wore a hooded sweatshirt, his face hidden by the shadow of the hood. I turned and walked in the opposite direction, my heart pounding in my chest. I had to find a way to get away from him. I looked around desperately for an escape route. I spotted an alleyway and decided to make a break for it. I ran toward it, my feet pounding on the pavement. The sound of the man's shoes echoed behind me, drawing closer with every step. A surge of adrenaline raced through me as I ran faster, my lungs burning as I gulped air.

The man was still following me, his footsteps reverberating off the walls of the alley. I felt his presence looming at my back. He seemed to move with purpose, as if he knew exactly where he was going. I quickened my pace and rounded the corner. This man seemed so professional, though—poised and focused, like he knew exactly what he was doing. He almost reminded me of a cop.

Just as I was about to reach the alley, I felt his hand grab my shoulder. I jerked away and turned my head, but I could only see a bit of his face where his hoodie had been partially pulled down. I couldn't make out his features clearly, but I was sure I didn't recognize him.

"What do you want?" I yelled, my voice trembling.

"Listen—" he started to say when suddenly a shout came from down the street. Ash was running toward me, his voice echoing through the air. As I stood there, trying to make a decision if I should run, the man sprinted away. I paid attention to what he was wearing, but it was just ordinary jeans and sneakers. He could be anyone. I wondered if he might turn around and run toward me again. But if so, he'd better think twice because soon Ash would catch up with him.

When I glanced to see if Ash had made it across the street yet, the man must have darted behind one of the buildings. He was gone. My mind raced. Why had he been following me? Was he the killer?

"What's going on, Madeline?" Ash asked as he ran toward me.

"He went that way. A man who was following me."

My arm trembled as I motioned in the direction he'd fled. Ash shouted something before he sprinted off after him, his gun drawn and ready for whatever was about to unfold. Fear gripped me as I watched him disappear from view. I wondered what I should do next. Just stand there and wait for Ash to return? But what if the stranger made his way back to me first?

Instead of continuing to stand in the alleyway where I felt vulnerable, I decided to hurry over to my car. I unlocked it and jumped inside, sliding behind the steering wheel and relocking the doors. I breathed a sigh of relief as I realized that I was safe. But the feeling didn't last long as I soon spotted a note on my car's windshield. I hadn't noticed the note when I had approached my car earlier, but now as I peered through the windshield, a knot twisted in my stomach. There it was, a white piece of paper tucked neatly under the wiper blade. I slowly opened the car door, feeling like I was walking into a trap. My movements were slow as I pulled the paper out from underneath the steering wheel. I cautiously opened the note, the paper crinkling in my hands. My eyes scanned the handwriting.

Scrawled onto the paper were the words:

Roses are red.
Violets are blue.

I see you.
Soon you will see me too.

Was the note from the same person who had killed Mallory? Or from someone else entirely? I felt a chill so cold that I thought I would never feel warmth again.

Chapter Thirteen

I clutched the note in my hand and got back into my car, locking the doors as I did so. My heart pounded as I peered out of the window, searching for any trace of the mysterious person who had left me the note. It felt like an eternity, but eventually I spotted Ash walking toward me. He was alone; it seemed that he hadn't been able to catch whoever had been following me earlier. I quickly rolled down the window and Ash leaned in.

"Any luck?" I asked, my voice wavering.

He shook his head. "No, whoever it was had too much of a head start."

"I had this note under my windshield." I handed it to him.

He took it from me and after reading said, "I'll find out what this is all about."

Maybe I was just being too paranoid, but he seemed pretty concerned. I had hoped he would tell me not to worry about the note, but he wasn't saying that at all. And the expression on his face made me worry even more. I needed to get on the case. As much as I trusted his detective skills, I couldn't just wait around for him to figure everything out. I had to try to find the person on my own.

"Do you have any idea who might have left the note for you?" he asked.

I shook my head. "No. Well, yes, I suppose maybe someone comes to mind."

He raised an eyebrow. "Who's that?"

I proceeded to tell him about Frankie and how he had a crush on me.

"So he likes cougars," Ash said with a smirk.

I frowned. "Is this funny to you?"

"No, of course not. But you're right—it's likely from him and just a teenage crush. Try not to worry about it, okay?"

I nodded. "Yeah, I'll try, but after Mallory's murder I'm a little on edge."

"Sure, I understand," he said. "Frankie's a good kid. He's probably just flustered by your pretty face. He's always been a little awkward."

I flushed and cleared my throat. "Well, I guess I should get going," I said.

"Will you be okay? Would you like for me to follow you home again?"

I shook my head. "That won't be necessary."

He tapped the side of the car door. "Not necessary, but I'll do it anyway, okay?"

"Yeah, okay, sure," I said, starting my car.

I realized that if anyone happened to see Ash following me home in his cruiser, then that would undoubtedly start rumors in town that I was an official suspect for the murder, being watched by the police. But I was ultimately glad that he had insisted on following me home. Not only did he follow me, but he once again walked me to the door.

I stopped at the front door after opening it. "Well, I guess I'm all safe now."

"You call me if you need anything. Anything at all. If something doesn't seem right," he said, searching my eyes.

I nodded. "I will."

He stared at me longer now. Why did it feel as if he wanted to kiss me? Suddenly there was a movement from over his shoulder. Ash spun around to see who was walking up the path toward my front door.

I was shocked to see who it was. James Laurent was looking right at me as he approached. James had the kind of good looks that could make a person stop and stare. He was tall, with broad shoulders and an intense blue gaze that seemed to take in everything around him. His dirty blond hair was slightly unkempt, and his strong, angular jaw gave him a rugged demeanor.

Yes, I said he was rather handsome before, but I had to be honest with myself right now—Ash was gorgeous. His intense blue-green eyes made me want to get lost in them. James, unlike Ash in his uniform, wore a stylish sweater and tight jeans. Actually, I'd never seen him dressed this casually. I had been used to seeing him at the restaurant or on a date, in a sharp suit and tie.

James smiled calmly, his expression a mixture of confidence and amusement. "It's good to see you, Madeline."

"James! What on earth are you doing here?!"

"I'm taking a course at a local winery, studying up on local varietals. All expenses paid by the restaurant and I get to stay out here for a bit. So of course I figured I'd drop by."

"Why didn't you tell me you were coming? And how did you know where I lived?"

"I wanted to surprise you. I was going to text you, but I overheard some locals mention your name at the vineyard and I spoke with them. And they told me where your new place was."

I recalled what Ash had said earlier, about everyone knowing everyone else's business in this small town. I also could only imagine that these locals, whoever they were, had likely been discussing my recent involvement in Mallory's murder case. I was suddenly a hot topic. But if that was true, it hadn't deterred James from looking me up.

Ash stood by silently so I felt I had to explain. "James and I used to work together back in LA. He's a sommelier."

"We did more than just work together, *non*?" James said playfully.

The air around all three of us seemed to crackle with tension. The men stared at each other for a few seconds but then focused back on me. What were they waiting for me to say? It didn't look like either man would budge off my front porch until I said something.

"Uh, it's good to see you, James." I felt Ash's stare on me. "When did you get into town?"

"Only a couple of hours ago. I wanted to come see you right away. You look great," he said.

"Not to interrupt this conversation," Ash said. "But, Madeline, you should probably get inside in light of what happened this evening."

I had a feeling he just wanted James to leave.

"What happened this evening?" James asked with alarm.

"She was accosted," Ash answered.

"Accosted?" James asked, aghast.

"More like approached," I said, cutting in. "Some guy followed me and grabbed my shoulder and then ran off."

"Did you catch the guy?" James asked.

Ash raised an eyebrow. "I'm working on it."

"Well, maybe Madeline shouldn't be alone," James said.

"She needs to get rest," Ash said.

"I think I can decide what I need to do. Thanks, guys. I'm going inside now."

I couldn't believe how they were acting. I really did just want to get inside and forget about all this stress for a while. Maybe I'd zone out in front of the TV. Or maybe I'd finally get to read some of that book I'd started.

"Good night," I said firmly, closing the door and leaving the men standing on the porch.

How long would they stand out there? I stood by the door for a couple of seconds and then looked out the peephole. They were just standing there staring at each other. It was clear that some kind of invisible power struggle was taking place between the two of them. A jittery energy skittered through me, but I didn't know what to do or say. They stood in the dim glow of my porch light, facing each other in tense silence.

As I watched, Ash gestured at James, his voice low and gruff. It was impossible to make out from inside the house what he'd said. James answered. Finally, after a couple more seconds, they both stepped off the porch. They stared at each other as they walked down the path and then away from my house. It was like they didn't want to take their eyes off each other to make sure the other one actually left.

Relieved, I stepped away from the door with dread still coiled in my stomach. I had no idea what would happen with those two, but I was glad it was over for now.

Chapter Fourteen

The sun was just beginning to rise as a group of customers gathered around the small table by the front window of my bakery. The aroma of freshly baked bread and pastries wafted through the air, mixing with the scent of coffee as they sat down to enjoy their morning treats. Business had oddly increased after the news spread of Mallory's murder. I still couldn't help but wonder if they were here for my pastries or just to find out more about the shocking event.

As they took their first sips of coffee and bites of croissants, one of the customers spoke up. "I can't believe there was a murder here."

The rest of the group, which included Natalie, immediately leaned in, eager to talk about the details.

"I heard it was the husband who killed her," another customer chimed in.

One of the older women spoke up, her voice steady and confident. "I heard it was some kind of contract killing," she said, her eyes scanning the room as she spoke. "I don't know the particulars, but rumor has it that the criminal had been hired to take her out."

That seemed kind of farfetched, but I supposed anything was possible. I thought of the man in the hoodie who'd approached me. Could he be some sort of hired assassin? Here in Solvang? I shook the absurd idea from my head.

"It's too surreal to even contemplate—a murder right here in our small town. We all usually felt so safe and secure, and now it seems as if all of that had been stripped away in an instant," said Natalie.

The gossip continued, just loud enough for me to hear: "Mrs. Johnson thinks it was Madeline. I mean, it happened right outside her bakery, and she had that big fight with Mallory at the baking contest."

They all looked my way, and I quickly diverted my attention so they wouldn't think I was eavesdropping. That Mrs. Johnson was just trying to stir up trouble.

"I can't believe it," gasped Beth Connor, who owned one of the many gift shops in town. "She seems like such a sweet girl."

"I heard Mallory was found in a pool of blood," said Mr. Miller. "Can you imagine? Someone sneaking up on her like that?"

The group shook their heads in disbelief and continued to speculate about who could have done such a thing.

"Well, let's think about this now," Natalie said.

Natalie had been a loyal customer ever since I opened up the bakery. She had supported me despite technically being a competitor, and she never asked for anything in return. Other than her briefly thinking I'd stolen her ingredients at the contest, we'd never so much as argued.

"Why would Madeline kill Mallory? Just because she accused her of stealing her éclair recipe? That doesn't sound plausible," Natalie said. "Madeline won the contest anyway."

At least Natalie was my friend again and was defending me.

"And Mallory was mean to everyone in town as far as I can tell. Doesn't that make us all suspects?" Natalie added.

"That's true. I do seem to remember you having a disagreement with Madeline at the baking contest, though. You were really mad," Beth said from across the table. "Mrs. Johnson said it turned out Mallory was the one who stole your ingredients, isn't that right?"

Natalie's face got red just like it had at the baking contest. She seemed to get heated at the mere mention of losing the baking contest. Then it hit me that I remembered that once Grandma Ruth had said she'd had an argument with Natalie about bringing dessert to the church's potluck dinner. Apparently the pastor had asked Grandma Ruth to bring dessert and Natalie had been highly offended.

"Oh, you can't seriously think I would kill someone over a baking contest," Natalie snapped. "And I apologized to Madeline for getting angry at her."

"Madeline had *more* of a reason," Mr. Miller said. "Getting accused of cheating is worse than getting some flour stolen."

I narrowed my eyes. I couldn't believe he'd said that. And after I'd given him a free pastry and coffee the other day.

"Mallory had been nothing but cruel to Madeline since moving to town and maybe this was her chance for sweet revenge," Beth suggested. "Something seemed odd about Mallory and Thomas."

"It sounds plausible to me," Mr. Miller added.

I let out an angry breath of air and then pounded my fist against the counter, sending a resounding thud throughout the room. I quickly ducked down behind the counter to hide and pretend I hadn't made the sound. The last thing I needed was for them to see me angry.

"I heard it was Ruth," said the first customer. "They had that big food fight and Ruth started it. She's always had a temper—remember when she threatened to tackle the visiting team's coach at homecoming?"

"I heard that people had never seen her so mad," interjected Mr. Miller.

The conversation continued on like that for a while, with everyone offering their own theories and rumors. As the group finished their pastries and coffee, they all agreed that they would have to keep their ears open for any updates on the investigation.

I'd be doing the same thing. No one was as motivated as me, since everyone was so wrongly focused on Grandma Ruth.

As they paused at the door to leave, Beth turned to the others and said, "I just hope they catch whoever did this. We can't have a murderer running loose in our town."

Their attention turned to me. This time I didn't look away. I didn't say anything about the comment. Instead, I said, "Thank you all for coming. See you soon, I hope."

They put on smiles and waved, acting as if they hadn't just been talking about me and Grandma Ruth, then went their separate ways. No doubt their minds were filled with thoughts of the tragedy that had struck our small community. It was on my mind too, and I had to do something about it.

"What will we do now?" Grandma Ruth asked. "We can't afford to lose customers."

I spun around, not realizing she had been behind me.

"How long have you been there?" I asked.

"Long enough to know what they were talking about."

"Everything will work out, Ruth," I said with a grimace.

"What's that look?" she asked.

"What look?"

"You know what look. You grimaced. You *don't* think everything will be okay."

"Of course I do," I said.

"You did it again. Stop doing that."

"Well, stop looking at me, then," I said, pretending to adjust the trays of pastries in the display case.

"We might as well hang the closed sign on the door thanks to me."

"Thanks to you? Mallory was mad at me, not you," I said. "It's not your fault."

"I started the food fight at the town hall," Grandma Ruth said.

"Well, we had customers today, so we have to stay positive that everything will be fine."

"How can we think that? There was a dead body by the dumpster," she said with a wave of her arm. "That's kind of a big deal."

I sighed. "Yeah, it's a really big deal."

The bell over the door jingled, announcing a new customer's arrival.

Grandma Ruth and I both looked up from behind the counter. Thomas walked in, his dress shoes clomping loudly on the tile floor. He didn't look like a grief-stricken widower. Instead, he looked angry. Unhinged, even.

I stiffened, gripping the edge of the display case as he stalked toward us. Grandma Ruth's expression was unreadable.

"Hello, Thomas," I said, keeping my tone neutral. "What can I do for you?"

He didn't answer right away, just stood there staring at me like I'd personally rolled Mallory in pastry dough and baked her into one of our galettes. His eyes were bloodshot, his face unshaven, and the tension rolling off him was thick enough to choke on.

"I think you'd be better off sticking to croissants and éclairs, *Madeline*," he finally said, his voice low and biting when he said my name. My real name. "Leave the rest to the professionals."

Grandma Ruth let out a quiet hum beside me but said nothing, her eyes darting between us like she was watching a soap opera.

"I'm sorry?" I asked, straightening.

He stepped closer, close enough that I caught the faint smell of whiskey on his breath. "You and your grandma seem real good at poking your noses where they don't belong. First in that baking contest mess, now in Mallory's . . . situation. Maybe it's time y'all learned to mind your business. Why did you come to my office pretending to be a private investigator? Using a fake name?"

The room seemed sharper and brighter with a nervous buzz, but I didn't flinch. Grandma Ruth had taught me better than that.

"Well, Thomas," I said, keeping my voice steady even though my palms were sweating, "considering we were the ones who found Mallory behind our bakery, I'd say we're already in the thick of it. Whether we want to be or not. I'm invested in uncovering the truth."

"But why did you pretend to be someone else"? His jaw clenched, and his eyes narrowed.

"I didn't think you'd talk to me otherwise, unless it was in some official capacity."

"I should report you! You don't know what you're talking about. Mallory was—" He stopped himself, shaking his head like he was brushing off a swarm of gnats. "Just stay out of it."

With that, he turned on his heel and stomped toward the door.

As the door slammed shut behind him, Grandma Ruth said, "Well. That man's wound tighter than a two-dollar watch."

I gave a startled laugh, breaking the tension. "Ruth, he just threatened us. Ugh, I shouldn't have gone to his office. That was so stupid."

"Oh, honey," she said, waving me off, "he's too scattered to anything foolish. Plus, I don't think he's got the guts to back it up. And if he does . . ." She reached under the counter and pulled out the rolling pin she kept stashed there. "I'll handle it."

I shook my head and started wiping down the counter. But in the back of my mind, Thomas's words still echoed. Whatever had happened to Mallory, he was hiding something. And I had a feeling it was only a matter of time before the truth came bubbling up like a pot of coq au vin.

Later that day, as I headed home, I tried to push the stress of everything out of my mind. But it was proving difficult. It had been a grueling day at work. My hair clung to my damp skin, and I couldn't wait to change into something more comfortable. I then had to take some time to plan my strategy for solving Mallory's murder.

I stumbled up the steps to my front door, my feet heavy with exhaustion. As I reached for my keys, something on the step caught my eye. It was a small package wrapped in brown paper and tied with a string. The paper was rough against my fingertips and faintly creased from being folded too tightly. A tiny note was attached to one end of the string, written in beautiful cursive handwriting.

I felt a mix of anger and unease. Could Frankie's crush on me have persisted despite my gentle rebuff? But then I remembered James's abrupt appearance, showing up right on this very doorstep, unannounced. Maybe this from him?

Taking a deep breath, I untied the string on the package and unwrapped the box. Inside, a potted succulent rested in its box along with dark crumbly soil. The plant's pink-tipped leaves were actually perfect for my windowsill garden.

Curiosity filled me as I unfolded and read the note:

Dearest Madeline,

You have no idea how much I admire you. I think you're smart, funny, and beautiful, and I hope you don't mind, but I left a small present for you in this package. I hope you like it.

The note was left unsigned. I carried the plant inside and set it on my kitchen table. As I admired it, I speculated on the sender. It was hard to tell, but the handwriting on this note seemed to match the one left on my car. Were these just romantic gestures that were being tainted by Mallory's murder, causing me to cast darkness on something sweet and innocent? But whether from Frankie or James or someone else altogether, I wasn't exactly thrilled with the attention. And why leave it all anonymous? Suddenly a new and even more troubling thought popped into my head: the man in the hoodie. Did I have a stalker?

Later that evening I lay in my bed, straining my eyes to make out the ceiling in the darkness. White specks fluttered around my head like snowflakes, each one melting away as soon as I tried to focus on it. I felt like I had been lying for an eternity, desperate for sleep but unable to find it. My pulse thudded in my ears as I looked around the room, every nerve in my body pulsating with fear. Were those really footsteps echoing through the house? I climbed out of bed and hurried over toward the door, desperately trying to prepare myself as I frantically listened for an intruder.

My eyes darted around the darkened room, and I heard a faint noise coming from down the hallway. My palms grew slick with sweat at the thought of someone being in my house. I cautiously made my way to the door, gripping the handle tightly before pushing it open and peering out into the shadows. The hallway was empty, but the noise still lingered in the air, barely audible yet enough to send waves of terror along my spine. Gritting my teeth, I stepped out into the darkness, hardly daring to breathe as I looked around frantically, searching for whatever had made the noise.

The strident sound of footsteps on wood drilled into my eardrums like a jackhammer. As I listened to the rhythm and timing of the tapping, the more convinced I became that they weren't just random noises from within the walls or some kind of strange insect. This was purposeful. Like someone walking through the house. Then a thud pierced the night air.

I wondered what to do. Should I go downstairs and investigate further? I didn't want to, but it wasn't as if I could just go back to sleep knowing something—or someone—was potentially in the house with me. Picking up the baseball bat I kept in the hallway closet, I tried to prepare myself for whatever I might encounter. Quietly, I eased down the hallway and peered over the banister into the hallway downstairs, which was dimly illuminated by the front porch light outside.

Taking a deep breath, I crept down the staircase, feeling along the wall for support. The shadows turned and moved as I passed, whooshing around me like cold winds stirring up leaves on an autumn day. I stopped at the doorway to the living room, unsure what exactly it was that waited for me inside the room. Holding my breath, I stood still and listened. But there was nothing there. Just the constant creaking that any old house made at night. I shook my head, telling myself it was just my imagination. But then I heard it again. It came from somewhere nearby. The creak of wood on wood and the soft tap-tap of something hitting against glass.

I gripped the baseball bat tighter and began to move again, trying to calm the butterflies in my stomach. I crept along the wall until I stepped into the kitchen, flattening myself against a wall as I waited for my eyes to adjust to the dark space. In the kitchen window I saw a figure reflected back in front of me. Messy, with wild hair and big eyes that stared back at me. I screamed until I realized it was my own reflection. I had a serious case of bed head.

That's when I realized that the back door had blown open. It was windy outside and I supposed I'd forgotten to lock the door when I'd taken out the trash earlier. I found myself wishing Pepper was with me tonight instead of visiting Grandma Ruth. I'd offered to arrange the visit in an effort to cheer her up after the last couple of stressful days.

After firmly shutting and locking the back door, I checked the rest of the house and windows. Everything seemed secure. But what had made the sound of footsteps? Or had that just been my imagination?

Chapter Fifteen

The sun was just beginning to peek through the clouds as Grandma Ruth and I made our way to church. Grandma Ruth had talked me into going, but I had insisted that we sit in the back pew. If I had to sit in front, I would feel exposed and vulnerable, with everyone staring at and whispering about us. I was certain they all thought we were somehow involved in Mallory's death beyond discovering her body.

Once we were inside the church, I admired how the sun shone brightly through the stained glass windows, the multihued light a kaleidoscope of brilliant color that illuminated the pews below. A cool breeze blew in from the open windows, dispersing the smell of candles and incense in the air. Grandma Ruth grabbed my arm and ushered me toward a pew. Thank goodness space was available at the back. I briefly thought of running out, but I didn't want to leave Grandma Ruth. As we shuffled into the pew, I couldn't help but notice the glances and hushed conversations taking place around us. I heard snippets of whispered phrases like "murderer" and "conspiracy," and it made my skin crawl. I wanted to find Mallory's killer badly. Maybe then people would stop talking about me and my grandma.

When we finally settled into our pew, I felt a wave of relief wash over me. Ensconced in the back of the church, no one could see my face clearly and perhaps everyone would forget we were there. Maybe that was wishful thinking. I took a deep breath and closed my eyes, trying to block out the whispers and focus on the sermon ahead.

Our fellow churchgoers sat patiently, their hands clasped together in prayer. The only sounds to be heard were the chirps of the birds outside, the occasional bark of a dog, and the rustling of hymnals as they were flipped to the correct page. The reverend stood at the front of the church, his hands raised in the air as he offered up a prayer. He spoke with passion, his words rising and falling like the waves of the ocean. As he finished the opening prayer, a hush fell over the congregation, a moment of reverence and awe—until the reverend suggested we take a moment's silence for Mallory. In that instant, people turned almost as one in their pews and looked back at Grandma Ruth and me. At the sudden rush of attention we remained frozen in our spots. In that moment I wanted to use my prayers to ask for a hole to appear underneath me so that I could disappear. As the sermon began, everyone finally faced forward again, and I let out a sigh.

After only a few minutes I felt someone staring again. I glanced over and spotted Mrs. Johnson squinting at us. I was pretty certain she wasn't supposed to judge me in the house of the Lord. Nonetheless, she gave a look that I knew meant she thought I should be ashamed of myself. Her words didn't need to be spoken for them to be heard. I felt my face flush and my stomach turn. I wished I could explain my side of the story to her, but I knew she wouldn't understand or want to hear. Instead, I kept my head bowed and my eyes lowered in a gesture of humility and reverence.

After the service I hoped we could slip out of the church without talking to anyone. I rushed Grandma Ruth toward the door, hoping to be the first ones out. We made it to the parking lot and were heading to my car when I heard someone call out to me.

"Yoo-hoo, Madeline!"

I groaned and stopped. I turned around and saw Suzette walking toward me. She had always been nice to me, though, so I waited for her to catch up to us.

Suzette gestured for Grandma Ruth and me to sit with her on a nearby bench. I glanced at Grandma Ruth and she merely shrugged. The three of us sat for a few moments as Suzette asked me about our well-being and said that we could always reach out to her if we ever needed someone to talk to. A few birds chirped in the background, and the sun's rays cast a golden hue on the parking lot.

"I heard you had words with Mallory before she was murdered," Suzette whispered as if she didn't want anyone to hear.

I was tempted to tell Suzette that fact was already all over town so there was no need to whisper. But instead I said, "Several times," I said. Talking about it made me relive the whole thing all over again.

Suzette nodded. "You know, this wasn't the first time she was involved in a baking competition scandal."

My eyes widened. "Really?"

"It wasn't exactly the same thing," Suzette said. "But it's definitely a pattern."

"How so?" Grandma Ruth asked.

"Over in Georgetown they had a baking contest. One of the contestants said that Mallory stole her recipe book. Mallory ended up winning that contest."

"Does she just go around to different towns and enter baking contests?" Grandma Ruth asked with a snort.

Suzette shrugged. "It sounds that way."

"How did you find this out?" I asked.

"I'm friends with the girl who had her recipe book stolen," Suzette said. "Um, when I told her about the murder, she recognized the name."

"Who is your friend? Can I talk to her?" I asked excitedly.

This was the first real clue I'd gotten. Maybe it would lead nowhere but it was a start. Suzette suddenly seemed to grow nervous.

"What's your friend's name?" I pressed, sensing that the conversation had changed course.

"Oh, well," Suzette said, looking away. "She might not want to talk about it."

"It's really important," Grandma Ruth said, trying to convince her to give us the information.

But Suzette only bit her lip and shook her head, still avoiding my gaze. Finally, she sighed and said, "It was me, okay? I'm the woman who she stole the recipe book from."

"Oh," I said in surprise. "Well, it's okay, I won't tell anyone."

"Needless to say, it was shocking to hear about her death," Suzette said.

"Can you tell me what happened at the baking contest?" I asked.

Suzette sighed. "Well, one minute she was being nice to me and asking about what I planned to bake. I told her about my recipe book. It had been my mama's. Anyway, the next thing I knew, I saw her in the parking lot around my car. I thought it was a little suspicious, but I didn't think too much about it until later when I went to get the recipe book and it was gone."

"So you left your car unlocked?" Grandma Ruth said.

She nodded. "It was a church parking lot. I didn't think anything of it. Who steals at a church event?"

"So then what happened?" I asked.

"Mallory won the contest—not surprisingly, since she made the best recipe from *my* recipe book. The one that I had marked as the one that I was going to bake. I didn't have the recipe memorized so I didn't get to be in the contest. And she won with *my* recipe!"

"Did you tell the police about this?" I asked.

"They didn't ask so I didn't know if it was relevant. I'd really rather stay out of it, if that's okay? I mean, I have no proof that she did it. Although I know she did."

"Sure," I said. "I understand."

"I hope they figure out who did this. I know you two had nothing to do with it," Suzette said.

"No, we didn't. Though she accused me of doing exactly what she did to you."

"No doubt she was guilty," Grandma Ruth said.

"After you won the contest that probably made her even more mad," Suzette said.

"She was livid," Grandma Ruth said. "Her face was redder than the ripe tomatoes at Mr. Sidebottom's roadside stand."

"Maybe she thought the best thing to do when she couldn't get the recipe from you and she wanted to win was to try to disqualify you by accusing you of stealing her recipe," Suzette said.

"I guess," I said around a sigh.

"Exactly my thoughts," Grandma Ruth said. "What a snake in the grass."

"Now, Ruth, we shouldn't talk ill of the dead. Not in the church parking lot," I chided.

"I suppose not," Grandma Ruth said. "But it still makes me angry. So I'll wait until we're out of the church parking lot."

"Is there anything else you can tell me about Mallory?" I asked Suzette.

She rose to her feet. "Sorry, I don't know much else. I hope everything gets better for you both soon."

"Thanks," I said.

Suzette murmured something about having to go. I could see the worry in her eyes as she'd spoken, and something told me maybe she wasn't telling me everything she knew about Mallory. As if she was afraid to say more. Grandma Ruth and I also got up to leave. As we walked toward my car, I glanced over at Suzette as she got into her car. I could tell that she was worried, but I didn't understand exactly why.

The sun was out in full force, and the birds sang loudly with joy, as if they were celebrating the day. Grandma Ruth looked out the car window and smiled.

"It's a beautiful day," she said. "We should go out and have a picnic today. It'll take our minds off our troubles."

I sighed and shook my head. "I'd love to, Ruth, but I have a murder to solve," I said. "I need to figure out who is behind this before it's too late."

Grandma Ruth nodded understandingly and patted my arm.

"Well, I suppose trying to tell you not to get involved in the investigation is pointless. You're clearly not going to listen to me. But for heaven's sake, if you must do this then, please, my dear, just remember you have to be safe. Don't wear yourself too thin. I know there's nothing I can say that will change your mind."

"It has to be done," I said. "You always told me that if you want something done right, you've got to do it yourself."

"You know you can't listen to what I say. I just say things to hear myself talk."

I laughed. "Well, nevertheless, I plan on finding the killer."

"Oh, sugar, your parents are going to ask me why I didn't stop you," Grandma Ruth said.

"Since when have you been able to stop me?" I asked.

"That's exactly what I'll tell them."

Chapter Sixteen

"Do you see him?" I asked Grandma Ruth, breaking our reverie. We'd been laughing together moments before, sitting in our car in the church parking lot. But then I'd suddenly experienced the now familiar sensation of being watched from afar. After a quick scan of our surroundings, I'd spotted him.

"See who?" Grandma Ruth asked as she looked all around.

"Look over at that oak tree across the parking lot, but don't be obvious."

Grandma Ruth quickly turned her attention in the direction I'd indicated. "That man over there?"

"Yeah," I said out of the corner of my mouth.

"Why are you talking like that?" she asked. "Are you having a stroke?"

"No, I'm not having a stroke, but I don't want him to know that we see him."

"Why not?" she asked.

"I think he's been following me."

"Does Ash know about this?" Grandma Ruth asked.

I locked my car. "I have no idea, but I intend on asking him."

"How do you know he's been following you?"

"He followed me the other night, but he bolted when Ash turned up." I suddenly made a connection that had been eluding me. "I think I saw him before too—the night Mallory was murdered. He was near the alley taking notes. He was wearing a hoodie then as well."

Now that I'd realized this mystery man had shown up at least twice before, and been nearby when Mallory was killed, it seemed even more serious. I dialed Ash's number, but he didn't answer.

"He's probably watching us because he thinks we're guilty," Grandma Ruth said, sounding a bit panicked.

I watched the man as I turned on the ignition. Would he follow us? I had a funny feeling that he would. He'd surely followed me to the church. Grandma Ruth gazed at the man by the oak tree. He was still there but seemed to be looking away. Was he really following us or was I just being paranoid? I didn't have time to think too much about it because suddenly he made a move toward his car at the far end of the lot.

My heart sped up as I watched him approach a bright blue sedan parked near the edge of the lot. He unlocked the car with a remote and got inside. Was he really going to follow us or was this all just a coincidence? I knew there was no way out of the situation without raising suspicion. If I sat much longer, he would think that I was up to something, so I put my foot on the gas and headed out of the church parking lot.

I drove down the street, the sun blazing hot in the sky, and as I looked in the rearview mirror, I noticed the blue sedan behind me. I tried to focus on the road ahead and not panic. Grandma Ruth sat in the passenger seat, her silver hair pulled into a tight bun and her hand white-knuckled against the car door. I didn't want to alarm her further, but the man's presence was definitely unnerving. As I pressed the gas, the engine rumbling beneath us, I felt her eyes on me.

"Don't go too fast in this traffic," she warned, her voice firm.

I knew she was right, but I wanted to put as much distance as possible between us and the blue sedan. I only hoped it would be enough.

I pressed harder on the gas as adrenaline buzzed in my veins. The man had been following me for the past few blocks, and I wanted to lose him before I reached the bakery. If I stopped at the bakery he might come after us once we got out of the car. We would have no way to get away. He seemed to sense my urgency; when I had picked up my pace, so had he. I glanced over my shoulder and saw that he was still there, keeping a steady distance between us. It was like he was a professional at this. As if he had followed many cars before.

I made a right turn and he followed, no longer trying to conceal his presence. Grandma Ruth, who was still clinging to the car door as if it was a life preserver, started to complain about my speed, but I ignored her. Up ahead, I saw a parking lot full of cars and an idea struck me. I would hide there. It was the only idea I had in my frantic quest to lose him. I veered into the lot and sped toward the back.

"What in blue blazes are you doing?" Grandma Ruth yelled.

Weaving in and out of the vehicles, I found an empty space and whipped my car in. I glanced in the rearview mirror, searching diligently for the man who had been following us. I prayed that I had managed to lose him, and so far there was no sign of his car. I breathed a sigh of relief, and headed out of the parking lot and back on the road.

"What's your plan now?" Grandma Ruth asked.

When I looked over, I saw her sitting there with her hands covering her eyes. Then she pulled a plastic bag out of her bag and pulled it down over her head.

"What on earth are you doing?" I asked.

"I can't handle seeing the traffic whiz by. If I'm going to die, then I don't want to see it happen," Grandma Ruth said.

"You're not going to die. I'm perfectly in control." I noticed that my hands were still clutching the steering wheel in a death grip. I loosened them a bit as we finally pulled up along the curb near the bakery. I quickly shut off the engine and glanced in the rearview mirror, relieved to see that the blue sedan was nowhere in sight. But he would no doubt find me again soon.

"How did you learn to drive like that?" Grandma Ruth asked, finally lowering her hands.

I didn't bother to answer her. Instead I dialed Ash's number again. When he answered, I hastily blurted out my new suspicions. "Do you want to tell me why the police are following me?" I demanded angrily. "I saw this same guy taking notes and talking to a cop the night of Mallory's murder."

I knew that the police, like everyone else, wanted to know if I'd killed Mallory. Or if Grandma Ruth had killed her. I looked over at my grandma. She was straightening out her hair after the paper bag had messed it up.

On the other end of the phone there was a beat of silence, then a deep exhale from Ash. "What are you talking about?" he finally asked. "The police aren't following you."

I chewed on my bottom lip, my mind spinning. I had been so sure a second ago that the authorities were on my trail, but now I wasn't. Could I have been wrong? Ash sounded surprised. Or was he just acting that way to throw me off?

"I assumed he was a cop. He followed me from church just now."

"Tell Ash the guy had beady little eyes," Ruth interjected.

Ash sighed again. "Look, I can't explain what's happening, but I think it's best if you just stay put for now," he said. "Are you at home or at the bakery? I'll come over and we'll figure this out together."

After I told him we were at the bakery, Ash quickly ended the call. Grandma Ruth and I waited impatiently inside for Ash to arrive. He stepped into the bakery only a couple minutes later, his eyes scanning the area for any signs of danger. He locked eyes with Grandma Ruth, her expression revealing a mixture of confusion, fear, and relief.

"Are you all okay?" he asked.

I nodded, my face softening from the tension I'd been holding in. At least some relief came over me in Ash's presence.

"We're fine," I replied. "But I want to know who that man was who followed us."

Ash nodded, his brow furrowing. "Tell me everything, slowly. With as much detail as you can both remember."

Between the two of us, Grandma Ruth and I described the man, the blue sedan, and what had happened starting in the church parking lot. Although Grandma Ruth wasn't quite as helpful, since she'd had a bag over her head for some of the time.

"I didn't make the connection until just now, but I realized I'd seen him before he came up to me on the street. I saw him briefly the night Mallory was killed, standing at the entrance of the alleyway with a bunch of other people. He was taking notes and nodded or spoke with one of the cops. I can't quite remember. But it was definitely him because he was wearing the same hoodie he had on when he grabbed me by the shoulder the other day."

"And then he followed you in his car just now," Ash supplied.

"Do you think this is the same guy leaving you those creepy notes?" Grandma Ruth questioned.

"I mean, the notes weren't necessarily creepy. They're like love notes. It's just the timing is weird, with everything else that been going on. But it's certainly possible they came from this guy," I said somewhat reluctantly. I still assumed the love notes and package had been from James. Maybe even from Frankie, but that seemed less likely. Something else was bothering me about the situation, but I couldn't crystalize the thought. My mind was still racing after the adrenaline of the car ride and the revelation that this mysterious stalker had been around the night of Mallory's murder.

"If you think of anything else, or see anything suspicious—heck, *smell* anything suspicious, just be sure to call me again. Immediately," Ash said as he strode toward the door.

"Can we send you home with anything? Some spandauers for the road?" Grandma Ruth offered.

"I'm still on duty," said Ash. "But thank you. Remember, don't hesitate to call me."

"Clearly we won't," I half joked. "I feel like we've had you on speed dial the last few days."

"Until we figure this all out—Mallory's killer, who this guy is who has been following you—we all need to stay on high alert." Ash was grimly serious; there wasn't a trace of humor in his voice or demeanor.

"We will," Grandma Ruth promised as she held the door open for Ash.

My eyes locked on Ash's broad shoulders and the confident stride that he seemed to carry with him everywhere. As he stepped out onto the street, I felt a strange pull in my chest.

When Ash turned back to look at me, our eyes met. He smiled softly and gave me a little nod before walking away. I blinked and he was gone, leaving me standing in the doorway, wide-eyed and, okay, flustered.

I noticed Grandma Ruth locked the door as soon as she closed it. "What's on your mind?" she asked me as soon as she turned around.

"What isn't?"

"I can tell your wheels are turning. And I'm not referring to your fancy driving back there."

"Something is bugging me. Something about those notes, ever since you mentioned them . . . but I can't put my finger on it. Not yet. It just reminds me of something."

"We both have been dealing with a lot the past few days. I know my mind has been scattered in a million different directions. Madeline, I've been meaning to say—there are some practical things we should discuss. About the bakery, and the house. Things we should sort out now, while we have the time. Paperwork and such. In case I have to go away."

"Where would you be going?" I asked but regretted it the moment I said it. She meant if she was sent to prison for a murder she didn't commit. With all the hubbub, it had been easy to forget just how vulnerable Grandma Ruth must be feeling. She was still the chief suspect, with the most evidence—circumstantial though it may be—stacked against her. And even so, her primary concern was making sure that I and the bakery were taken care of.

"Ruth," I half whispered. "How did things so wrong, so quickly?"

"I don't know, kiddo," she said, "But until we're able to figure all this out, I don't know if we'll ever feel safe in this town again."

Chapter Seventeen

When in doubt, I baked. Even though it was Monday and the bakery was closed, I decided to channel my nervous energy into productivity. I had been baking for a few hours when I finally felt the stress of the day start to lift. Baking was always a therapeutic experience for me, allowing me to forget about the worries and fears that had been weighing me down. Grandma Ruth kept me company as I worked. The kitchen was filled with delicious aromas—the sweet smell of cake, the warmth of the freshly baked bread. The scents surrounded us, a comforting hug of familiarity. I was so content in the moment that it felt like my worries had melted away.

As we finished, Grandma Ruth reached into her apron pocket, pulled out a package, and handed it to me. I opened it to discover a beaded necklace with a charm in the shape of a star.

"I keep forgetting to give this to you. Your great-grandmother used to wear this," Grandma Ruth said, her voice full of love and tenderness. "I want you to have it now. It's a good luck charm. Heaven knows we could both use some good luck right around now."

"Ruth, it's beautiful."

I remembered seeing my great-grandmother wear the necklace, though she'd moved on to heaven when I was just a young girl. Tears welling up in my eyes, I took the necklace from Ruth and hugged her tightly.

"Now, don't get too mushy on me. We've got work to do and no time for crying." Grandma Ruth started moving pots and pans to the sink.

I had a feeling she was keeping busy so that I couldn't observe her emotion in the moment. I knew that this had been a gift not just of the physical object but of the memories and stories associated with it. And in that moment, I finally felt at peace. The feeling didn't last long, though. The sweet moment of my grandma giving me a gift was interrupted when a noise came from outside the bakery's back door again.

Grandma Ruth's face went pale as she grabbed my arm and quickly whispered, "What if it's that strange man again? What if it's the killer? We should call Ash."

"He only just left here a couple of hours ago!" I whispered back. I wanted to stay with Grandma Ruth in the safety and warmth of the kitchen, but I thought I needed to find out what was going on out there myself. Maybe it was nothing, and I hated to bother Ash yet again.

Grandma Ruth grabbed my arm as I started to head toward the door. "Where are you going? I don't think it's a good idea for you to go out there. Ash told us to call him right away if anything suspicious happened."

I thought about all the times as a kid I'd ignored her advice and done the opposite of what she'd said. This time was no different—I didn't listen. I was getting sick of running to Ash every time something happened. I wanted to accomplish something on my own, whatever the risks involved. I was tired of being at the mercy of all of these unknown forces and unseen threats. I raced to the back door with nerves crackling like live wires. I had no clue what kind of danger could be lurking outside, but I was fueled by pent-up anger from the last few days.

With an iron will driving me forward, I prepared for whatever challenge awaited me. Sweat trickled down my forehead as I grasped the handle, and I prayed that whatever lurked on the other side wouldn't be strong enough to overpower me. Taking a deep breath, I twisted the doorknob and steeled myself for whatever might come. My heartbeat thundered in my ears as I stepped out into the alley from the back of the bakery.

"This isn't a good idea," Grandma Ruth called out from behind me. "Why won't you listen to me?"

I squinted against the bright yellow light cast by the sun. The air was thick and heavy with the smell of something sweet and putrid, like rotting fruit. My forehead beaded with sweat as I inched forward, my eyes searching desperately for any sign of movement. The silence was deafening. Every nerve in my body screamed a warning.

I inched down the alleyway, my every sense on alert. Fear coursed through my body like an electric current. Suddenly I heard something, a sound like a gasp or a whimper. I stopped dead in my tracks. I was sure there was a person lurking somewhere nearby. A chill ran down my spine.

"Get back in here," Grandma Ruth said from the doorway, breaking the silence.

Just as the fear started to overwhelm me, a small shape emerged into the bright sunlight. A cat strolled from the shadows, white with gray stripes. It stared right at me and let out a low meow. I released a deep breath, my heart still pounding in my chest.

"Will you get back in here?" Grandma Ruth called out.

"It's just a cat! Nothing to worry about," I said.

The cat blinked at me, unperturbed. In a moment, the fear I had felt began to melt away, replaced by a strange sense of calm. I watched as the cat crept toward me and gently rubbed its furry head against my leg before turning to head back down the alley. A smile crept onto my face as I realized I had been letting my nerves get the better of me.

Right before I reached the door, though, suddenly I heard it again, the same strange noise I'd heard earlier. Was it the cat again? It seemed too loud and to be coming from farther down the alley. With nervous energy rushing through me, I turned around cautiously, my feet making barely a sound on the pavement. I tried to keep my breathing steady, though my fears were rising with every passing second. What was the source of the noise?

As I walked down the narrow cobblestone path, my mind was full of thoughts about the danger waiting for me at the end of the alleyway. Then suddenly I saw a figure approaching me out of the corner of my eye. Was I about to be attacked again? I spun around and threw a punch at the man as he got close. He grunted and then grabbed his face. In that moment I realized I'd hit James.

"Oh no," I gasped, my eyes widening in shock. "I'm sorry. Are you okay?"

James shook his head, a slight smirk on his lips. "Yes, I'm all right. But you sure do pack a punch."

I stood in stunned silence as I stared at James's familiar face. What was he doing back here? His tall frame and chiseled features only further accentuated his strong presence. His tousled hair and swagger gave him a suave, intriguing air.

"What are you doing back here in the alleyway, James?" I asked.

James gave me a rueful smile, the kind that said he wished he had a better answer. "I came back here to find you," he said simply. He paused for a moment, and I could see a multitude of worries written on his face. "I came back for you," he said again, more softly.

My stomach tumbled with butterflies as my mind spun in disbelief. I couldn't believe it. "Why?" I finally managed to ask.

"Because you're irresistible." James took my hands in his and gazed into my eyes. "I missed your éclairs."

"Stop playing around," I said.

"Well, and the restaurant sent me out here to learn more about local vineyards," he said with a grin.

"Most people use the front door when they come to visit," I said sharply. "I came out here because I heard a noise, but it turns out it was just a cat. And you."

"I can understand why you'd be nervous after what happened," he said, touching my cheek gently.

"Since you're here, would you like to come in for an éclair?" I asked, gesturing over my shoulder.

"Yes, I'd like that, Madeline," he said and his French accent made me melt like butter on a croissant.

As we approached the back door, Grandma Ruth looked James up and down.

"Oh, well, look what the cat dragged in," she said flatly.

"This is my . . . friend, James," I explained. "We knew one another back in LA."

"I remember you mentioning him," Grandma Ruth said, but there was a curious tone to her words.

"He came by for an éclair," I said.

"I'll just bet he did," she said sarcastically. Clearly, Grandma Ruth was rooting for Ash.

As James followed me through the kitchen to the front of the bakery, Grandma Ruth trailed behind us.

"So you two used to work together?" she asked.

"*Oui*. But we also dated," James explained.

"Well, dated as in had two dates," I was quick to clarify.

"Those must have been some dates, for you to follow Madeline all the way up here," Grandma Ruth stated.

"Indeed," James said dreamily, watching my every move as I pulled some éclairs out from the refrigerated bakery counter. "I was so excited when the opportunity arose to come out here to the vineyard and I realized I could also reunite with Madeline."

"Which vineyard is it again?" Ruth pressed. But James ignored her and just kept watching me with a dopey look on his face.

I'd originally intended for James to sit and eat in the bakery, but his behavior was making me rather uncomfortable. And Grandma Ruth was clearly not any happier with his presence than I was. So instead of placing the éclairs on a plate, I slid them into a to-go box and tied it shut with string.

"Here you go," I said, handing over the box.

James looked down at the box in his hands confusedly. "Oh, I thought that we might—"

"We're closed," Grandma Ruth said.

"We've got a lot of work to do before we reopen tomorrow morning," I said.

"Ah, well then. I'll come by again soon," James said.

"I'll see you out," Grandma Ruth said, leading the way back through the kitchen.

"Until next time," James said, casting a smile at me over his shoulder as he departed.

Suddenly exhausted, I dropped into the nearest chair and waited for Grandma Ruth to return.

"I don't know what you ever saw in that guy," she said as she reentered the room. "He's got about as much charm as Pepé Le Pew."

"We only had a couple of dates," I reminded her again.

"All the more reason why it's odd that he'd travel all this way to see you."

"I'll choose to not take that as an insult. Firstly, he only traveled a couple of hours, and it was for a vineyard, not for me. Besides, am I not a compelling enough reason to come visit?"

"You know what I mean. It's just seems too neat, that he shows up during all this hubbub to take a wine class. And he certainly doesn't seem all that busy, for having come up here to 'study.'" She made aggressive air quotes around her last word.

She was making some valid points—but then again I didn't want Mallory's murder to make me paranoid. Not everyone had double motives and secrets to keep, even if it seemed that way lately.

"How did you even first get together?" she asked.

"Oh, he—" I began but then caught myself as something suddenly clicked in my head.

"What? What is it?"

"He left me a note."

"So?"

"He left me a note. On my car outside the restaurant," I said slowly.

"Just like the note you found the other day?" Grandma Ruth said quickly.

"Not exactly the same but . . . it's weird, right? Could it just be a coincidence?" I fiddled with my new necklace as I tried to sort out my thoughts. "But I mean, even if James is the one leaving me those notes, there's nothing inherently sinister about them. Other than the timing, coming close after Mallory's murder. But he doesn't have any connection to Mallory."

"Or does he?"

Grandma Ruth's word hung in the air, yet another unanswered question added to the mix. The questions were continuing to stack up, but the answers remained maddeningly elusive.

Chapter Eighteen

I was rather well known for my relentless need to fix things when I thought they were wrong. I needed to find the person who had killed Mallory. The whispers and fingers pointing around town at me and Grandma Ruth seemed to be intensifying. I had compiled a list of suspects. Even though other people might only have a slight motive, I'd still added them: Thomas, Suzette, even Natalie. I felt bad about putting some of them on my list. Like Natalie. Sure, she had been angry at Mallory, but was she really capable of murder? And there was one person I refused to add to the list, even with a motive: Grandma Ruth.

She seemed more nervous than usual, overcharging one customer before realizing her mistake and then nearly dropping a tray of croissants as she placed them in the display case. The stress of recent events and being one of the chief suspects in a murder investigation was inevitably weighing on her—just as it was on me. I needed to take action, to feel like I was making progress with my investigation, such as it was.

I decided to go back to Thomas's office. I made some lame excuse to Grandma Ruth about needing to go pick up some baking supplies and hurried out to my car. During the drive over, anticipation coiled inside me. Doubt and fear consumed me with every step as I made my way out of the parking lot and into the building. What if Thomas called the police on me this time? My entire body shook at the thought of being arrested. What would Ash say if he knew about my little visit? No doubt he wouldn't be happy. I couldn't tell him what I'd done. I had to keep this a secret. I wouldn't even tell Grandma Ruth because she would also freak out.

The receptionist watched me as I entered. I felt her gaze burn into my back as I stumbled away from the main door. Her typing had abruptly quieted, and she seemed intent on tracking my every move. There was no escaping her watchful eye. At least she hadn't called security on me. Yet. I moved my feet faster, figuring if I moved swiftly enough and with a sense of purpose she would think I belonged there. My breathing was heavy, adrenaline pushing me forward while dread followed close behind.

Panic welled up inside me as I desperately cast my eyes around the room for somewhere to hide. Spotting a gnarled ficus tree at a corner spot in the hallway, I dashed over and pressed myself behind its prickly leaves, hoping it would be enough to conceal me. Thank goodness a solution had presented itself because I had been running out of ideas. The tall plant offered the perfect cover. Though I hoped no one would see me hiding back here, if anyone recognized me, they would think I was bonkers. The wacky French bakery owner.

How had I gotten myself into this situation? I was so thankful that Ash didn't know about this. I strained to listen for any hint of the receptionist's whereabouts but heard only a menacing silence. I peeked out from behind the large ficus tree. No one was in the hallway, so I eased out from behind the tree and to the corner of the hallway. I peeked around the edge. The receptionist had stepped away from her desk. But for how long? My mind raced with an endless stream of possibilities.

I knew I had to get a look at everything on top of and in Thomas's desk, but how could I do it without him knowing? Could I sneak into his office? I'd been good at sneaking out of places but never good at sneaking in. Since I'd called ahead and asked, I knew he wasn't in his office at the moment, but what if he returned while I was going through his things? Or what if the receptionist had lied when I called earlier?

I had to take my chances. I raced out from behind the tree and sprinted down the hallway to his office door. I prayed that the door wasn't locked. Fumbling with the doorknob, I finally got the door open and slid inside. I rushed inside with no regard to the alarm bells ringing in my head. I moved quickly across the room but paused when I thought I heard a noise. Freezing on the spot, I held my breath and listened for several seconds. There was nothing; it must have just been someone passing by the door. But I knew I had to hurry. I took a deep breath and slowly eased closer to the desk. The room was quiet and dim, the only light coming from the window. With every muscle in my body tense, I slowly approached the desk.

I wasn't even sure what I was looking for, but my plan of action was to snoop around the top of the desk and drawers, then search around the rest of the room for any clues. The desk was cluttered with an array of items. Desperately, I ran my hands across the surface, frantically shifting objects as I rummaged for something, anything that could prove a lead.

My searching felt like it took an eternity, yet I'd found nothing. I frantically scanned the desk, pushing papers and objects around with frenzied determination. With every item I moved aside, I hoped I was closer to uncovering an answer. My eyes strained as I searched for a hint, a clue, something that would unlock the mystery of Mallory's death.

I'd still failed to find anything significant when I spotted several pieces of paper, all neatly arranged at the corner of his desk. I carefully shuffled through them, trying not to make a sound. I found an insurance policy, and I quickly snatched it up. It was for Mallory, and I felt my heart drop as I realized this could be the evidence I had been searching for. I remembered Suzette saying that Thomas had taken out a life insurance policy on Mallory only recently. Could her husband have been so cold-blooded as to murder her for money? I shuddered at the thought.

I didn't have much time to ponder this before I heard footsteps again in the hallway. Quickly, I tucked the policy into my pocket and started rifling through the desk drawers, which were thankfully unlocked. I knew I shouldn't be snooping around like this, but I didn't see any other way to find out what I needed to know. I somewhat hoped that I wouldn't find anything further against Thomas because I didn't want to believe he'd kill his wife, but at the same time, a part of me was desperate to uncover the truth. I didn't want Grandma Ruth or myself to end up in jail.

Finally, I spotted something tucked away in the back corner of the drawer. It was a stamped and addressed envelope but unsealed. Inside was a white piece of paper, folded in half. I carefully unfolded it and read the words written on it in neat handwriting:

Dear Sophia,

I hope this letter finds you well, although I must admit that my current state of mind is far from calm. I'm very upset. I have a heavy heart, and I needed someone to talk to about what I found. I know we talked today and you sensed something was wrong, but I just couldn't express how I felt. That's why I thought I would just write a letter. You've always been such a dear friend and offered the best advice.

As you know, I always felt like Thomas and I had a strong bond of trust and understanding between us. We have weathered countless storms together and celebrated the joys of life side by side. However, now I'm not so sure about our bond. Recently I discovered something that has left me feeling deeply hurt and betrayed. It pains me to even put this into words, but I found that my husband has taken out an insurance policy on me without my knowledge or consent.

The shock of this revelation has left me reeling with a mix of emotions. How could he make such a decision without even discussing it with me, his partner and equal? It feels as if I'm nothing more than a financial transaction. I thought we were a team, making decisions together, and now I find myself questioning the foundation of our relationship.

I understand that insurance policies are meant to provide security and protection, but this feels like a violation. It raises questions about how my husband perceives me and the level of trust he places in our relationship. It is disheartening to think that he would take such a significant step without considering my thoughts, wishes, and concerns.

Perhaps my husband had good intentions and saw it as a way to ensure my well-being in case of unforeseen circumstances. However, the lack of communication and transparency has left me feeling excluded and marginalized in a matter that affects me profoundly.

Having said all that, I feel like I know what advice you'd give. Maybe that's why I wrote all this down—just to work through all my thoughts. You would tell me that I need to have open and honest communication with him. And you'd be right. I intend to address this issue directly with Thomas. I's crucial for us to have a sincere and heartfelt conversation where I can express my feelings and seek clarity on his motivations. I hope that through dialogue, we can reach a deeper understanding of one another and rebuild the trust that has been shaken.

In sharing this distressing news with you, my dear friend, I seek solace and support. Your friendship has always been a beacon of light in my life, and I trust that your empathy and wisdom will help me navigate this challenging situation. I value your perspective and would greatly appreciate any insights or advice you may have to offer.

Thank you for being the compassionate confidante that I can turn to in times of need. Your presence and understanding mean the world to me, and I am grateful for the strength you lend me with your unwavering support.

With love and gratitude,

Mallory

I hadn't expected to find something this significant. This letter from Mallory about her husband shifted my perspective. I had harbored negative feelings toward Mallory due to her erratic behavior. However, as I read her heartfelt and sincere words, I realized that there was more to Mallory's story than I had initially assumed. Maybe I had been too quick to judge her based solely on her outward behavior. Though she *had* attacked me and my shop for no reason. But the letter had revealed a depth of emotion and vulnerability that I hadn't anticipated, making me reconsider my initial impressions. In my rush to defend Grandma Ruth, I had overlooked the fact that another woman had lost her life, violently.

Despite Mallory's past actions, I began to empathize with her on a deeper level, recognizing that everyone had their own struggles and complexities beneath the surface. The discovery of the letter made me approach Mallory's memory with a greater understanding and compassion. It was as if Mallory had spoken to me from the grave, pleading with me to find her killer.

I pulled out my phone and snapped a photo of the letter. I consider taking it with me, but I couldn't prove that I'd found it in Thomas's office. I wouldn't even be able to prove that Mallory had written it. I wondered why it was unsent. Had Thomas intercepted it and prevented it from being mailed out? Or had Mallory simply failed to send it before her death, and then he discovered it?

Finding the insurance policy along with this letter was certainly incriminating. And the policy was for a sizeable amount. Did Ash know about this? Surely, he must have; he was a good detective. That was partially why I knew he'd be offended if he discovered I was trying to solve the crime myself.

I stood in Thomas's office, nerves sparking through me while I scanned the room for anything else. Fear gripped me as I imagined Thomas catching me snooping through his belongings. I made my way to the window and peeked through the partially open blinds. My stomach dropped as I spotted Thomas's car, unmistakable in the sea of vehicles. But what caught my eye next froze me in place. There he was, sitting in the driver's seat, with a woman beside him. My breath caught in my throat as I watched them, disbelief washing over me.

They were kissing. A total make-out session. After his wife had just died. It was unbelievable.

My mind raced with a million questions, but one thing was clear: Thomas was having an affair. The realization hit me like a ton of bricks. This, along with the insurance policy, certainly gave him quite the motive, no doubt about it. But now another puzzle presented itself. Who was this mystery woman? How could I find out more about her? My thoughts whirled as I struggled to come up with a plan. One thing was for sure—I needed even more answers now, and I wasn't about to let this affair go uninvestigated.

Chapter Nineteen

When I stepped out of Thomas's office, I almost expected the receptionist to be waiting at the door for me. Thankfully, she was nowhere to be seen. Then the sound of the elevator doors opening caught my attention and I spotted the receptionist coming out of the elevator.

I couldn't just stand there and wait to be discovered. Without thinking, I raced down the hallway in the opposite direction. Adrenaline coursed through me as the sound of my footsteps echoed off the walls. I had no plan and no idea how I would get out of the building without being spotted. As I rounded the corner and looked down the hallway, I saw an exit door just ahead of me. I figured it must be for the stairs. I'd have to take them down instead of the elevator. My legs moved faster and faster until I was almost sprinting toward the door. I grabbed the door handle and yanked it open. All I knew was that I had to get away—fast.

Going down five flights of stairs wasn't my idea of fun, but it was my only way out. I bolted down the stairwell, my feet pounding the steps like cannonballs. Desperation drove me forward, but fear of being caught kept my movements jerky as I lurched from one flight to the next. The walls blurred around me as I sprinted down the stairs, my heart racing faster than my feet. I felt like I had been running forever, but I knew I could not stop.

At last, I reached the bottom of the staircase. I stumbled outside and into the warm air, taking deep breaths of relief. I was safe, for now. I had made it out. And maybe with proof that Thomas had killed Mallory. I hurried across the parking lot, relieved that no one had followed me. Luckily Thomas was in the parking lot on the other side of the building. It seemed I'd pulled off this little escapade, and I was actually kind of proud of myself. Now I just needed to make it back to my car. I didn't dare breathe as I watched the door of the office building. When I was sure the coast was clear, I made a dash for the edge of the parking lot where my car was and finally stopped running.

I took a moment to catch my breath and gather my thoughts before heading off again toward my car. I smiled in relief, feeling my heart rate slow. As I turned, I immediately felt something smack against my face. I gasped for breath as I stared into the eyes of the handsome man I'd smacked into. The shock of the moment rooted me to the spot.

"What are you doing here, James?" I asked, curiosity and embarrassment in my voice. I had smacked right into his chest, and when I looked up into his mesmerizing eyes, my heart skipped a beat. Still, I couldn't help but wonder how he seemed to be everywhere but the vineyard where he was allegedly taking classes. He kept turning up like a bad penny.

He smiled in response, displaying perfect white teeth. "I came to talk to my friend," he said. "He works here now."

If that was true, could James find out more information about Thomas, my number one murder suspect? Maybe there was some office gossip his friend had told him. Any help I could get would be appreciated.

"What are *you* doing here?" he asked.

"Um, delivering a catering order." I gestured over my shoulder. The fact that I'd come up with that lie so quickly was a little scary. I was getting better at this stuff. I didn't want to lie to James, but I felt it was totally necessary in the moment.

"Well, it's great to see you. I didn't get to talk to you the other day as much as I'd wanted," James said, his eyes scanning me intently. "Your grandma seemed to want me to leave. And maybe you did as well?"

"We've just got a lot going on at the moment," I said awkwardly, thinking back on the connection I'd made between the note he'd left me back in LA and my recent secret admirer.

"Ah, well. Would you like to have dinner with me? If you've got any time in that busy schedule."

James's question caught me off guard in more ways than one. Ash's face shot through my mind, and I felt a sharp pang of guilt for even considering his invitation. James waited patiently for my answer, his gaze still fixed intently on mine. I was hardly in the mood for a date right now, but if James had a way of getting more information on Thomas, it could work in my favor. This was my choice, and I had to make it.

I took a deep breath and finally replied, "Sure. I would like that."

"How about tomorrow night at eight? I'll pick you up."

I nodded. "Sure, that sounds great."

"Perfect," he said with a smile.

Now I had something else to ask him, changing the subject from a dinner date to helping me solve a murder. "Can you help me with something?" I asked, trying to sound as casual as possible.

He nodded, his face illuminated in a soft orange glow from the setting sun. "What do you need help with?"

"The murder victim's husband works here. Maybe your friend could tell me more about him. I want to figure out if he killed his wife. His name is Thomas."

James had a funny look on his face and didn't respond.

"What's wrong?" I asked. Was I asking too much of him?

He exhaled deeply, running his hand through his hair. "Thomas is the friend I mentioned who works here," he said.

I hadn't seen that coming. Now James probably wouldn't want to help. Plus, I didn't want James to tell Thomas that I had been snooping around.

James seemed to be in a state of shock, as if struggling with how to proceed. "What do you need to know about him? I know his wife was killed near your bakery. I didn't want to say anything because I know it has to be difficult for you."

"I don't want Grandma Ruth, or me for that matter, to end up in jail accused of her murder," I said tartly.

"They don't seriously think you had anything to do with her murder, do they?"

"I don't know what they're thinking, but I can't take any chances. Look, I know he's your friend, but what can you tell me about his relationship with his wife? Do you think he could have killed Mallory?" I asked.

I also wondered if I should break it to James that his friend was having an affair. Or did he already know? I looked at James, trying to read his body language and see if he was hiding something or could offer some insight. His expression told me nothing; it was now an inscrutable mask. He took a deep breath and let it out slowly before speaking.

"I don't know," he said. "I can't be sure, I mean, I know they had their differences, but I don't think he would do something like that." He shook his head. "But I guess we can never really know anyone entirely. Do you suspect him just because he was her husband?"

"No, of course not," I said.

I could tell he was struggling with his own emotions, trying to make sense of what I was telling him. I felt for him; this wasn't easy for anyone, myself included.

"I don't know what happened, I just don't know. All I can tell you is that Thomas is my friend. But I can't be sure what happened between them," he said.

"I'm sorry to make you even consider it . . ."

James shook his head and managed a weak smile. "No, it's all right," he said. "I just need some time to process everything. I'll talk to you about it more over dinner tomorrow?"

"That sounds good," I said, feeling slightly disappointed. But I'd welcome another opportunity to ask him more questions. Now that I knew James did indeed have a connection to Mallory, his sudden presence in Solvang felt more suspicious than ever.

James paused before saying, "But you should investigate if you think it's necessary. Maybe Thomas can help you figure out what happened to his wife." He seemed genuine in his offer to help with my investigation—unless he was interested in leading me down the wrong track and away from him.

"I'm sorry," I said softly. "I didn't know you two were friends. I don't want to cause you any trouble."

He touched my arm. "You're never going to cause me trouble. I want to help you, Madeline."

"Then there's something I need to tell you."

"What is it?"

"Thomas was having an affair. I saw him kissing another woman just now," I blurted out.

His eyes widened. "Are you sure?"

"Of course I'm sure. I wouldn't make that up," I said with a frown.

"Of course not," he said.

"Did you know about this?" I asked.

He sighed. "No. I knew he had become close with someone else, but he assured me there was nothing romantic between them."

"So you know who she is?" I asked.

He nodded. "Her name is Allison Gibbs. She works at the bookstore in town."

"Well, I just hope this gets solved soon. Thank you for everything. I have to go, but I'll see you tomorrow."

I knew the next step in my investigation would be Allison's bookstore. I could either find her there and speak directly or there might be someone else who could talk to me. As I walked away, I looked back and saw James standing in the same spot, his gaze distant, lost in thought.

Chapter Twenty

As I walked into the bookstore where Allison worked, a restless thrum was just under my skin. The Book Cottage was just that—a quaint little cottage on a street corner filled with new and used books for sale. I scanned the front room nervously, searching for Allison among the shelves and stacks of books. I was a bit frustrated that rather than narrowing down my search, my list of suspects was continuing to grow. If Allison was truly having an affair with Thomas, that would certainly provide her with a motive for wanting Mallory out of the way. But maybe it wasn't a bad thing that the suspects continued to stack up—the greater the number of suspects, the less focus on Grandma Ruth and myself. Either way, I needed to learn more.

And then I saw her, standing behind the counter, flipping through a stack of papers. Allison was a striking woman, with dark hair that cascaded down her slender shoulders. She had piercing green eyes that seemed to hold a thousand secrets. There was a tension in her posture, a nervous energy that I couldn't ignore.

Taking a deep breath, I approached her. "Allison?" I said, my voice trembling slightly. "We need to talk."

Of course she probably had no idea who I was . . . or did she? She must obviously know about the murder.

She looked up, her eyes widening in surprise as she saw me. "Madeline," she said, her voice cautious. "What brings you here?"

So she did know me. The plot thickened. Then again, I was quite recognizable these days, with my picture on the front page of the local paper and my name a hot topic around town.

I didn't waste any time beating around the bush. "I saw you," I said bluntly. "With Thomas earlier. In his car. Kissing."

Allison's expression faltered for a moment, a flicker of guilt passing across her features before she regained her composure. "Madeline, I—" she began, but I cut her off.

"I don't want excuses," I said, my frustration boiling over. "I want the truth. How long has this been going on?"

Allison sighed, her shoulders slumping slightly. "It's been going on for months," she admitted, her voice barely above a whisper. "Thomas and I . . . we'd been seeing each other behind Mallory's back."

My mind reeled at her words, the pieces of the puzzle finally clicking into place. Thomas's affair . . . Mallory's erratic behavior . . . But as anger on Mallory's behalf surged through me, I knew one thing for certain—I wasn't going to let them get away with this.

I fixed my gaze on Allison, my eyes boring into hers with intensity. "Did you or Thomas have anything to do with Mallory's murder?" I asked, the words tumbling out of my mouth before I could stop them.

Allison's eyes widened in shock, and then her expression hardened, a defensive edge creeping into her voice. "How dare you even suggest such a thing?" she spat, her voice tinged with anger.

But I refused to back down. "You had a motive, Allison. And Thomas . . . his affair with you . . . it all adds up."

Allison's jaw clenched, her hands balling into fists at her sides. "You have no proof of that," she hissed, her voice low and dangerous. "And I won't stand here and listen to these accusations."

My own anger rose in response to her denial. But despite the heat of the moment, I knew I had to stay focused. Mallory deserved justice, and I was determined to find the truth, no matter what it took. Without another word, I rushed out of the store. That hadn't gone as well as I had hoped. I should have kept my cool before confronting Allison, but it was too late now. What was done was done.

Chapter Twenty-One

I stood in the entrance of the bakery, the morning sun pouring in from outside. My heart felt heavy, and I had a sudden urge to turn and walk away. But then I spotted a white envelope on the ground. My name was scrawled across the front in unfamiliar handwriting.

I hesitated before I nervously picked up the envelope. With trembling fingers, I opened the envelope and unfolded the paper inside. It was written in French, and although my French wasn't perfect, I could make out most of it. And the words were chilling:

Meet me at the crooked windmill at two. Don't take this lightly and don't tell the police. There will be pain if you do.

I frantically tried to figure out who could have sent such a note, and why. The only French person I knew was James. I knew I had to go to this meeting to find out. I slowly got up, my knees shaking. I walked back to the kitchen, still clutching the paper. I had to be brave and face whatever was waiting for me.

I quickly prepped the kitchen and opened the bakery, my hands continuing to tremble as I did so. I tried to stay focused on my job, but I couldn't help but think about the mysterious note. I had to know who the sender was and what they wanted.

At two, I locked up the bakery and headed to the windmill just as was written on the note. There were actually several well-known windmills in town, the most photographed being the one in the heart of town. But the crooked windmill was more of a local site than a tourist destination. It was part of an old restaurant that had closed in the 1980s and remained abandoned ever since. Time and weather had done a number on the place, causing the small tower to lean. Everyone just referred to it as "the crooked windmill," and it was a spot where teenagers would gather at night to drink in the parking lot—at least, based on the number of bottles I spotted as I pulled my car up to the tiny parking lot with cracked pavement.

After I opened my door and stepped out, I darted my eyes around for any sign of the person who had asked me to meet them here. The windmill loomed in front of me, the afternoon sunlight shining around the rotating blades. A couple of tourists were around, taking selfies or simply checking out the unusual structure. But I noticed nobody out of the ordinary, and no one seemed to be paying attention to me. Yet I couldn't shake off the feeling that someone was watching me.

I felt a jolt of adrenaline course through me when I saw a figure standing near the tower, their face turned away. The figure stepped slowly forward, revealing themselves to be an elderly man with a poodle on a leash. He was rather hunched over and shuffled more than strode. His dog seemed as elderly as he was, keeping slow pace with the man.

"Uh, hello? Did you perhaps leave this note for me?" I asked, showing him the paper.

The man stared back at me, confusion in his eyes. "What's that, young lady? Have we met before?"

"I don't think so. I was told to come here to meet someone . . ."

"I was just walking Viking here," the man gently tugged on the poodle's leash. "And he followed his nose over from the sidewalk to sniff around."

"Oh, I must have been mistaken then. I'm sorry to have bothered you," I said, embarrassed by this wild goose chase. My confusion grew as I slowly made my way back to my car. The air seemed to grow a little cooler, and the shadows cast by the trees appeared darker, more ominous. My thoughts were interrupted by a friendly and familiar voice.

"Hey, Madeline! Fancy seeing you here," Natalie greeted me with a smile, as she paused on the nearby sidewalk.

"Hi, Natalie." I hesitated for a moment, since Natalie was technically still on my list of suspects. But she was pretty far down the list, and I needed to vent about this latest strange occurrence. "You won't believe what just happened," I began, recounting about the strange note I'd received and my brief encounter with the old man.

Natalie listened intently, her expression growing thoughtful. "That sounds suspicious. Maybe someone wanted you out of the bakery."

"That hadn't occurred to me," I said, and the thought of someone luring me away from the bakery raised even more unsettling questions. "I should run, Natalie. It was nice seeing you."

"You too. Stay safe, Madeline."

I quickly made my way toward my car. I figured I should get back to the bakery—fast. But I formed a new plan as I headed away from the windmill. When I arrived at my destination, I could hardly keep calm. I pulled up in front of Thomas's house, a modest white two-story house fronted by a manicured lawn in a suburban neighborhood. Suzette had mentioned the address more than once, and I'd made a point to remember it. I'd decided to go to Thomas's house instead of returning to the bakery because he had skyrocketed to the top of my suspect list since I'd learned about his affair with Allison. I figured he was still probably back at his office.

The afternoon sun glared down with blinding intensity, searing the air and burning away any hint of clouds. The heat was oppressive and relentless, wrapping the world in a shimmering cloak of yellow light. I stepped out of my car and walked up the driveway, my footsteps the only sound in the quiet neighborhood, its occupants either at work or content to remain indoors and avoid the heat. Even the birds had fallen silent, leaving only an eerie stillness.

A for-sale sign was stuck in the lawn. Did Ash know that Thomas was selling, perhaps planning to leave town? Once up the front porch steps, I hesitated for a moment before knocking, unsure of what I was even doing. To my surprise, the door opened almost immediately.

"Madeline! What a surprise! Are you here for the open house?" asked Suzette.

I nodded and forced a smile. She had no idea my real reason for being here, but I'd gotten lucky. "Yes, that's why I'm here."

"I figured you wouldn't want to rent forever. This place is a real gem." Suzette stepped aside. "Please come in."

I felt a bit wary, as I didn't want Thomas to know I'd been snooping around his house. Could I trust Suzette to keep her mouth shut?

"Suzette, I hope you can keep it quiet that I'm house hunting. I, uh, don't want Grandma Ruth to know. She thinks it's too soon for me to consider buying a house. You know, until the bakery gets off the ground more."

"Oh, mum's the word! Keeping secrets comes with the job. You have no idea the things a real estate agent sees and hears! But let's get to it! The house has three bedrooms and two baths," Suzette said. "As you can see, the living room is quite spacious."

I was on edge as I gazed around the room, looking for something, anything, that could be a clue. The inside of the house was neat and orderly.

"The owner . . . he's moving out of town?" I asked. I hoped she didn't get suspicious that I'd brought him up.

Suzette stared at me for a moment before answering. "Oh, Thomas. Yes, he's moving soon. He didn't say where he's going, though. But obviously it must be hard being here, with talk all over town and all the memories connected to the place."

"Yes, it must," I said nervously.

She looked around as if someone might be listening and then said in a lowered voice, "I'd heard rumors about Mallory's deteriorating mental state. People say that she suffered from an undiagnosed mental illness."

"Yes, I'd heard about that too." Suzette was proving quite the gossip—which was all the better for my investigation.

We moved about the house. When we reached the primary bedroom, I couldn't help but notice that it seemed to be devoid of any sign of Mallory. No personal items, no pictures, no shoes, no purses. I made my way across the bedroom to what I assumed was the closet door when Suzette piped up again. "It has lovely closet space."

I twisted the doorknob and opened the closet. There was nothing much in there either—none of Mallory's clothes and seemingly very few of Thomas's as well. It was as if he had already packed up. I remember seeing the half-packed suitcase in his office earlier.

"Since you've spent some time with him, what do you think of Thomas?" I asked as we walked out of the bedroom.

She shrugged. "I don't know what to think. At one point he suggested Mallory's death might be related to the baking contest."

I almost tripped over my own feet. Of course she'd heard that rumor. I shouldn't be surprised. It was time for me to get away. I hurriedly trailed Suzette down the hallway, my eyes absorbing the pictures of Thomas's past life that hung on the walls. He seemed to stare back at me, like his eyes were peering into my soul. Being in this house was making me anxious. And so far I'd failed to find any solid clues that would unmask the truth about his wife's untimely demise.

Suzette finally stopped in front of a large portrait of Thomas and Mallory. Mallory looked beautiful, with flowing hair and a delicate, porcelain face. She was younger in the photo and looked happy—unlike how she'd seemed in the days leading up to her death.

"She was quite beautiful, don't you think?" Suzette said quietly.

I hurried across the foyer, my heart racing as I tried to make sense of the little that I'd learned so far. At the front door, Suzette said, "Let me know if you'd like to make an offer. I think the house will sell quickly."

"Oh, sure thing," I said with a smile. "Absolutely."

I wanted to tell her to contact me if she heard anything else about Thomas and the murder, but that would seem weird. Besides, she probably wouldn't hear anything. Only more gossip, no doubt. It wasn't like Thomas was going to confide in her and confess to murder. Although that would make things a lot easier for me.

As I left the house something felt off, and it wasn't because I'd been in the home of a potential murderer. I once again had the feeling of being watched from afar. I hurried back to my car. Would leaving really do any good, though? If someone really wanted to, they clearly could just follow me as they had been doing. Nevertheless, staying around certainly wasn't going to help, so I quickened my steps.

Chapter Twenty-Two

I *knew* someone had been watching me. I glanced over at the house next to Thomas's. I saw no one outside, but perhaps someone was watching me through a window, wondering who their potential new neighbor might be. I looked around at the other houses and all remained quiet. It seemed as if hardly anyone was home. Certainly a bad day for an open house, but what did I know? But then I caught sight of movement again, and I looked across the street at the house to the right.

I glimpsed someone, but the figure darted around the side of a neighboring house. I could barely make them out before they disappeared from view. I had no idea if it was someone I knew or a total stranger. There was only one way to find out. My inner detective sprang into action. With an air of determination, I sprinted across the street, dodging a passing minivan like an Olympic athlete. I stumbled blindly around the corner of the house, only to come face-to-face with a woman wearing in a large straw sunhat and wielding an old garden rake.

Her eyes blazed with anger as she exclaimed, "What on earth do you think you're doing?"

I realized that I had mistakenly trespassed on her property. Well, not mistakenly. I'd only mistakenly gotten caught.

"Sorry about that," I said as I hurried around her.

"Where are you going?" she demanded.

I didn't respond as I dashed around her azalea bush and into the next yard. Sensing the climax of my pursuit, I closed in on the guy, ready to confront him. He had no idea that I was standing behind him. He stood at the edge of the property and was looking down at his phone. With my heart beating fast, I tapped him on the shoulder, causing him to jump in surprise and drop his phone, which promptly tumbled into the nearby bush.

"Gotcha!" I exclaimed triumphantly. "You've been following me this whole time!"

"Actually, ma'am," he replied with a bewildered expression, "I haven't been following you. I have no idea who you are and why you're in my yard."

My face turned beet red with embarrassment as the man stared at me. Keeping my gaze fixed on the ground, I apologized profusely and reached under the bush to retrieve his phone. As soon as it was safely back in his hand, I mumbled another apology before fleeing from his yard.

Once back on the sidewalk, I quickened my pace and for a brief moment felt relieved. But that sensation was quickly extinguished when I reached my car. Fear tightened in my chest at the sight of a sheet of paper tucked under the windshield wiper. I took a deep breath and slowly walked around to the driver's side door. While I had been out chasing strangers in their own backyards, someone had been tracking me. Was it the killer? Was it James? Were they one and the same? Or was it the mystery man in the hoodie? I also realized I was right outside Thomas's house, and Suzette had been nearby as well. Once again, the number of suspects felt unwieldy.

I stared at the paper, knowing that I had to read it, even though I didn't really want to find out what it said. I took a few moments to steel my nerves before finally reaching out to grab the paper. My hands trembled as I unfolded the sheet. My stomach dropped as I saw my name written in large, blocky letters. Something told me this wasn't an invitation to a tea party. The words were once again all in French. What I couldn't read I typed into my phone for translation, revealing the message in full. This note was much longer than the previous one. I wasn't sure if it was due to the translation, but the language was also rather florid and formal—and certainly dramatic.

> *Madeline Andersen: I write this letter as a warning, a plea to spare yourself from delving deeper into the abyss. Leave behind the desire to uncover the truth, for ignorance can be a savior in the face of the unspeakable horror that could befall you.*
>
> *I'm in the shadows now, but I will step out if you don't stop. Some secrets are best left undisturbed. Each step forward will reveal a breadcrumb of evidence, enticing your curiosity further. But beware, for the breadcrumbs pave a treacherous path leading not to redemption, but to a dreadful revelation that may consume your very essence. Madness lurks in the tendrils of each revelation, threatening to ensnare your mind, leaving only fragments of the person you once were.*
>
> *The face of the murderer is veiled in darkness, shrouded in mystery. Leave it that way. The blood-stained hands of the wicked should never be your burden*

to bear, lest you find yourself forever trapped in a web of despair.

I beg of you, heed this warning. To investigate this murder is to invite your own undoing, and my wrath upon you. Retrace your steps, retreat into the light, and let this mystery remain forever unsolved.

Remember, dear Madeline, the abyss stares back when one dares gaze into its depths. Spare yourself the torment that awaits those who unravel the threads of this dark tapestry. May you find solace in ignorance, for in this realm, ignorance truly is bliss.

Yours sincerely,

X

A chill ran down my spine as dread engulfed me. Was this note from the killer? I quickly glanced around to make sure no one was watching me before scanning the contents of the letter again, trying to make sense of it. As I finished reading it for the second time, I decided I had to ignore the warning and find the killer. I wouldn't let someone intimidate me. Yes, it was dangerous and maybe a little crazy, but I felt as if I had no other option.

The sudden shrill sound of my phone ringing pierced the silence. Startled by the interruption, my hand shook as I swiped to answer Grandma Ruth's call. Her number glowed like a warning sign on my phone's screen. Warning me not to do anything stupid. Well, it was too late for that.

"Hello?" I said whispered into my phone. I was even more on edge than I'd realized.

"Why are you whispering? And where are you? We have baking to do."

"I'm on my way," I said, hoping that she didn't sense the fear in my voice.

"Where are you?" she repeated.

"I'm on my way," I said again.

"You're purposely avoiding answering my question, which means that you're doing something you shouldn't be doing. I can hear it in your voice. Now you get over to this bakery right now and stop whatever nonsense you've got going on," Grandma Ruth barked.

"Yes, ma'am," I said. "I'm coming."

"And no stops along the way."

"Yes, ma'am," I said again.

"All right then. Well, be careful," she said in a slightly less agitated tone.

As I pulled away from the curb after saying goodbye to Grandma Ruth, I glanced in my rearview mirror and spotted a black Toyota sedan. The driver had pulled up along the curb in front of Thomas's house.

I waited to see what the driver did next. The car door opened and Thomas got out. Since when was he driving a Toyota? Instantly, I flashed back to the scene of Mallory's murder, that night in the alleyway. I'd found the key fob to a Toyota. It couldn't be a coincidence that Thomas was now driving a Toyota. What would he have said if he'd come back and found me in his house? Thankfully I wouldn't have to worry about that particular scenario. I sat there for a couple of minutes, tapping my fingers against the steering wheel. Seconds later Thomas emerged from the house holding a piece of paper in his hand.

With seemingly not a care in the world, he strode down the front path and hopped back into his car. I decided in that instant to follow him, despite the promise I'd just made to Grandma Ruth to return to the bakery. Thomas started his car and headed down the street in the opposite direction. I was relieved, as I wouldn't have to turn around or worry about him driving past me.

Without hesitation, I pulled away from the curb and began tailing him down the street. If he realized I was following him, then there was no telling where he would go. He'd probably lead me to the police station and tell them that I was following him. And that I was potentially the killer. Something told me he hadn't noticed me, though.

This was definitely a dangerous move, but at this point, I was in too deep. I couldn't back out just because things were getting dangerous. I had to push forward. Of course Grandma Ruth would not be happy with me, but what she didn't know wouldn't hurt her. Although she had a way of finding things out. I still wasn't sure how she did that. I'd never been able to fool her with anything for too long.

I kept careful watch on Thomas, tracking every turn he made and making sure to maintain just enough distance so as not to be spotted. Adrenaline surged through me; I felt like a true private investigator on a surveillance mission. The longer I followed him, the more I started to feel that I was uncovering something dark and sinister. Maybe he was leading me to the piece of evidence I'd need to finally solve this case. After about five minutes or so of trailing him, Thomas parked his car in front of an old warehouse. I watched as he went inside.

After just a couple of minutes, he stepped out of the building, his face now ashen and sweat beads across his forehead.

His eyes were dark and vacant. He shuffled over to his car and opened the trunk with a metallic click. He grabbed a long, black bag and slung it over his shoulder before making his way back inside. Outside of the sound of traffic along the street, the area seemed particularly still, as if it were holding its breath. I looked to see if anyone else was around. In the distance I noticed a parked car. Was Thomas was meeting someone?

It was time for me to find out what was going on inside that building. I approached the dank old warehouse, its massive windows boarded up with plywood. My heartbeat quickened as I neared the crumbling old building. I crept forward toward the main doors. My anxiety mounted as I opened the unlocked door and stepped inside, feeling the chill of damp concrete and broken glass crunching beneath my feet. Mustering all my courage, I crept farther inside. I knew there were potentially things I would regret seeing, things I did not want to encounter. I prayed that I wouldn't once again be witness to something I'd never be able to forget, like the discovery of Mallory's murder.

The only sound came from the steady drip-drip from a broken pipe, the water staining the walls a dull shade of gray. I could see dust motes suspended in the air, illuminated by a thin beam of light that shone through the tiny window at the far end of the room. I walked toward the back of the warehouse and suddenly a noise came from somewhere close by. I froze on the spot, my eyes struggling to adjust to the darkness as my heart thudded in my chest. I waited in the shadows, not daring to move, as I listened to the unmistakable sound of a voice coming from the far corner of the room. As I strained to make out the words, as suddenly as the talking had started, the person, presumably Thomas, stopped speaking. But there was no other sign of him.

I spotted a closet door in the darkness and, without hesitating, jumped inside and pulled the door closed behind me. I stood motionless in the cramped darkness. The air felt even staler and damper in the enclosed space. It was like breathing through a musty rag. As I shifted my weight, something poked sharply into my leg. I heard footsteps as they thudded against the floorboards outside the closet, moving closer and closer. I held my breath, knowing that if whoever it was managed to spot me, my fate would be sealed. I let out a silent plea for mercy, hoping against hope that I would remain hidden.

Peering through the small gap between the closet door and its frame, I saw a female figure, her pale face illuminated by the dim light of the warehouse. I held my breath, waiting to see her next move. She had no idea that I was watching her. Where was Thomas? Was she looking for him too? The woman's black silk dress rustled as she moved across the room. She paused for a moment, and then kept going, the sound of her echoing footsteps gradually fading away. I waited a few moments longer until I was somewhat confident that I was alone. I then slowly opened the door and stepped out of the closet.

I squinted through the dim light, trying to make out any signs of life—hoping that the woman had in fact left. Where was Thomas, anyway? Just as I was about to leave I saw something in the corner of the room. There was a single sheet of paper lying on the floor, illuminated by the pale sliver of light streaming through a crack of the boarded-up window. I carefully stepped over to it, wary of any loose floorboards. I knelt down to see what the note said. I wondered if this was the same paper that I'd seen Thomas holding earlier.

The page was creased and wrinkled, as if it had been wadded up and tossed in the trashcan only to be fished out again. The handwriting was nearly illegible. I had to squint to make out the words, which read:

I write this letter as a warning, a plea to spare yourself from delving deeper into the abyss. Leave behind the desire to uncover the truth, for ignorance can be a savior in the face of unspeakable horror that might befall you.

It was word for word what had been written on the note left on my car earlier, only this time in English. The only thing missing was my name. Had Thomas written it? It was almost as if this had been his practice sheet. But why would he have brought it with him inside this building? Now I had even more unanswered questions. I decided the best thing for me to do was leave while I still could. I wanted to get out of the warehouse alive. I scurried down the long hallway and almost immediately spotted Thomas. He had his back to me and hadn't noticed me. Yet. I hoped to keep it that way.

I quickly ducked behind a large column, pressing my body against its cold surface, hoping to avoid detection. After a few seconds, I couldn't help myself. I had to know what was going on, so I peeked out from behind my hiding spot. Thomas hesitated for a few moments, looking around him cautiously as if he was also checking for any signs of danger. Was he looking for the woman? Or did he sense that I was around? I watched him take out a small envelope from his pocket. He glanced around one more time before walking to the front door of the building. He paused and then slipped the envelope back into his pocket.

Thomas loomed by the door, his shadow stretching out a monstrous hand. His silhouette seemed to grow longer and wider as he shifted his weight from one foot to the other. I held my breath, heart pounding so hard it felt like it might escape my chest at any moment. Every fiber of my being screamed at me to run, but I was trapped. The only thing I could do was watch him. Seconds later, Thomas walked out and slammed the door shut behind him with a thunderous crash, leaving me standing there in the silence. As I inched closer to the exit, a tight pressure built in my chest and sweat started to drip down my temples. If he returned now, it would surely be too late, so I made a break for freedom.

The sound of a door slamming shut behind me was like a cannon blast, reverberating through my entire body and leaving me momentarily paralyzed with panic. I knew I had to run quickly so I forced myself into motion toward the door, my breath coming in short gasps of fear. The hallway seemed to stretch out before me in a long, winding tunnel, but I pushed onward, determined to get out alive. I imagined Thomas standing by the door once I got outside, ready to pounce.

When I reached the door, I threw it open. Quickly I looked to my left and to my right. Thank goodness no one was there. As I burst out of the building, my eyes struggled to adjust to the harsh sunlight. Through a shimmering haze, I caught sight of Thomas getting into his car. Panic clawed at my throat. Should I follow him again? Was it worth risking everything just to satisfy my curiosity? With my heart still pounding, I took a deep breath and rushed into the parking lot. I had been lucky this time not to be caught, but I knew I had to be more careful in the future. Well, I hoped I didn't have to snoop in the future. But never say never.

My legs moved faster, carrying me toward my car before I could even think twice about doing anything else risky . As I reached out to grab the car handle, I worried deep down that this was only the beginning of something much darker and more dangerous than I could have ever imagined.

My breath seemed to come quicker now, as if the decision I had made was somehow pushing me forward with an urgency that had nothing to do with me and everything to do with solving this crime. The sun was lowering in the sky, but the heat was still oppressive. A strange determination seemed to come from some place deep within me.

Heat pressed down on me, turning the car into an oven. My palms slicked against the steering wheel, slipping just enough to make me tighten my grip as I trailed Thomas. I was no longer thinking about the consequences. My body ran on instinct as I followed his car, weaving in and out of traffic. I was barely aware of the sights and sounds around me. My thoughts spun with possibilities, desperate hopes, and desperate fears. What would happen if I caught up with him? Where was he going? What secrets would I uncover if I followed him all the way to wherever he was headed? I needed to know if he'd written the note. Every second dragged as I drove. The only thing that filled my mind was the urgent need to know the truth about the note.

I tailed him until he'd arrived at his destination, my foot pressing heavy on the accelerator and then slamming on the brakes Thomas's Toyota roared up to his house and screeched to a halt. He sprung from the vehicle like a wild animal. He didn't even notice my car. I'd kept close behind him, although I'd been careful to remain out of sight. Even now that he'd stopped moving, he still had no idea of my presence, unaware that he had been hunted.

Once he was out of sight, and without a plan, I rushed toward the front door of the house, my feet pounding on the pavement with each step. All was still, maybe eerily calm. Sunlight glimmered off the grass and made its way through the branches of the tall, stately trees that bordered the property. My gaze settled on a small piece of paper, lying in the center of the porch. Had it fallen out of his pocket? I stood over it for a moment, my hands trembling as I reached down slowly to pick it up. In that moment, I wondered if this would be the clue that finally solved Mallory's murder. Could I be that lucky?

My hands finally stilled as I unfolded the note, my eyes scanning the words quickly. I'd been expecting more incriminating words, but instead it was a blank sheet. Seriously? Apparently, I hadn't been that lucky. Though in that moment I realized with a sinking feeling that it was exactly the same type of paper used for the threatening notes I'd received. This had to be more than a coincidence. Not wanting to confront Thomas and hoping he hadn't noticed me following him home, I rushed off the front porch. Exactly what had I gotten myself into?

Chapter Twenty-Three

I raced away from Thomas's house and hurried toward my car, eager to be away from the dangerous situation. But as I sprinted down the sidewalk, I spotted a familiar figure standing in the shadows by a house at the corner. Frankie. He must have seen my expression change, because he stepped out of the shadows and into the sunlight. Now I could make out all of his features. His dark eyes watched me intently, as if he was challenging me to confront him. He then turned and acted as if he hadn't even noticed me. I wouldn't buy into that act, though. The sun was starting to set and the tall oaks that lined the street billowed their leaves as if they were signaling a warning to me. Thankfully, the air was also getting cooler as dusk approached. I couldn't handle all this stress and the heat at the same time.

When my phone dinged I almost jumped out of my skin. I yanked the phone from my pocket and saw it was a text from Grandma Ruth.

Are you alive?

Call you soon, I quickly typed out.

My nerves sparked as I watched Frankie now hurry away from me. I hadn't expected to catch him in the act again, and it was clear from his body language that he hadn't expected to be seen either. He had been trailing me for days, and I had had enough.

I thought for a moment of chasing after him again. Though I was kind of exhausted from all the chasing. Nevertheless, I decided I had to confront him and see if his appearance here was a coincidence or not. My feet moved of their own accord and I started after him again, my exhaustion forgotten as my fury propelled me forward, but he'd gone around a corner, and by the time I got there, he was gone.

I thought about calling the police. And I probably should have. Though what would I say? Frankie hadn't actually done anything, I was just on edge. I had no proof that he'd been following me. I marched straight toward my car, determined to get to the bottom of this. I knew where Frankie lived with his parents. I would go there and inform them about their son's suspicious behavior.

I fished my keys out of my pocket and got into my car, slamming the door shut behind me. I turned the key in the ignition and the engine roared to life. I sped off in the direction of Frankie's house. The small white house with blue shutters sat at the end of the shady street where Grandma Ruth also lived, just a few doors down. The green lawn was lined with lavender along the sidewalk, flanking roses that grew on either side of the front porch's steps. A boxwood wreath hung on the carved wooden front door. The light hung low in the setting summer sky, painting everything in a watercolor wash.

As I pulled up outside the house, I noticed the faint glow of a light on in the front room window. Someone must be home. I didn't see Frankie's car parked anywhere nearby. To the right stood an oak tree, so massive and old you couldn't guess how many years had passed since it first took root. I got out of my car and marched up the driveway. Once up the front steps, I knocked sharply on the door and, after a few moments, it opened cautiously. Frankie's mother appeared in the doorway, her eyes widening with surprise when she saw me.

"Madeline! This is a surprise."

"Mrs. Castille, I want to talk to you about your son."

She opened the door wider and motioned for me to come in.

I didn't hesitate in explaining exactly why I was there. "I think that Frankie has maybe been following me," I continued. "And I think he has been leaving me notes and gifts. Some pretty disturbing notes, actually."

She eyed me up and down. Based on her expression and body stance, I was pretty sure she wasn't happy with me. Her face was an inscrutable mask. She didn't seem angry, per se, but she didn't seem pleased with me either.

After a beat of silence, she spoke. "You say he's been following you?"

"That's right," I said.

"If what you say is true, then I'll make sure he understands that this behavior is unacceptable." Mrs. Castille paused, her lips pursed in thought. I braced myself, not knowing what to expect next. I sensed that she didn't truly believe me.

"I would appreciate that," I said.

"He has mentioned that he has a crush on you," she said, her tone measured and even. "That's not something I can turn a blind eye to. I want you to know that I take this matter seriously. I need to be sure that my son understands the seriousness of his actions and that he behaves with appropriate respect." Something about Mrs. Castille's demeanor seemed off.

"I'm sorry I had to come to you with this," I said.

"Yes, well, I apologize for any discomfort this has caused you," she said in a clipped tone. "I want to hear any concerns you may have, so that I can address them and ensure that my son respects you."

Just then, Frankie walked through the back door, his typical white T-shirt sweaty and his jeans grass-stained. His face was blotched, like spots of maroon paint colored his skin. The screen door slammed as he rushed inside. He stopped in his tracks when he saw me. Our gazes locked and a flicker of fear flashed through his eyes.

"Frankie, Ms. Andersen says you have been bothering her? Do you want to tell me what's going on?" his mother asked.

His only reply was a panicked look before he bolted away from us and back out the door. The screech of the screen door's hinges cut through the air as it vibrated wildly in its frame before coming to a shuddering halt. A loud echo reverberated around us, signaling the finality of his escape.

Mrs. Castille turned to face me again. "Well, I'm so sorry, but it looks like he's just being a teenager."

I stared at her for a moment, shocked at her dismissive words. "I understand he's a teenager, but this is bordering on stalking. And I really wish you would have a talk with him about this."

"Maybe you're imagining things."

"I'm not imagining the gifts and notes he's left me."

"I'm not sure I really see the problem," she said.

"At first, I thought nothing of it, but I think he's been following me. Everywhere I go lately I have the sense that someone has been a few steps behind me."

"And my Frankie has said bad things to you?" she asked.

"Well, no, he hasn't approached me directly or said anything. But I can feel eyes on me." I realized I was starting to sound a bit paranoid. I didn't have a lot of evidence to back up what I was saying.

She frowned. "How do you know he is following you?"

"Well, I've seen him and I'm just afraid of what he will do if this infatuation goes unchecked."

"Boys will be boys. I think you are blowing this wildly out of proportion," she said.

Clearly, she wasn't going to do anything about this.

"Fine, I understand if you don't believe me, but regardless he needs to stay away from me. I just wanted to make sure that you were aware of the situation," I said. "Please ask your son to stop."

"Your concerns have been noted."

The talk hadn't gone as well as I had hoped. Now Frankie's mother thought I was lying to her.

"I don't want to have to go to the police," I added.

She studied my face for a moment before she said, "I heard what happened at the bakery."

"Which part? The fact that a woman was murdered or that they haven't found her killer yet?" She was making me angry.

"Well, I heard that *you* found the woman." She looked at me suspiciously.

"That's right," I answered.

"You and your grandma found her."

I didn't like the way that this conversation was going. If she wasn't going to talk to Frankie, then perhaps it was time for me to leave.

"Thank you for your time. Again, I'd appreciate it if you'd talk to your son. Please tell him to leave me alone. Thank you." I turned on my heel and walked out the front door.

Chapter Twenty-Four

After speeding away, I drove back to Thomas's house like a bat out of hell, determined to get the answers I was looking for. I still needed to call Ash, but in the moment I wanted to confront Thomas.

With my hands trembling slightly and my legs a little shaky, I marched right up to Thomas's front door and knocked. I waited anxiously for him to answer. His eyes widened in shock when he saw it was me. He must have still thought I was a private investigator. My mind raced as I held his gaze, bracing myself for what could possibly lie ahead.

"I'm sorry to bother you, but I just have some more questions," I said.

"Well, you certainly are bold, aren't you?"

"It's the only way to get to the bottom of things, don't you think?"

"I suppose," he said.

He wasn't asking me to come inside and that was fine. I'd already been in the house once and that had been enough.

"I was wondering if you knew anything about a recipe book. Someone claims that Mallory stole their recipe book."

"That's preposterous," he said. "She would never do anything like that. And I knew my wife well."

Did he?

"Who accused her of that?" he demanded.

"That doesn't matter."

"It does matter if she's they're accusing Mallory of something. Maybe that's why she was killed."

"Well, that's what I'd like to find out," I said.

"I don't know anything about a recipe book."

"The woman says it was taken on Sunday morning from her car at church, on the seventeenth."

"Well, that can't be possible because Mallory and I were at breakfast that morning. We decided not to go to church and have a nice quiet breakfast. I even have a receipt from where we went and text messages about it." He pulled out his phone and, after scrolling for a minute, showed me messages between him and Mallory coordinating the plan.

"So you weren't living together at the time?" I asked.

"Well . . . no. She'd moved out. We were having troubles. Difficulties, but we were working through it."

"Right," I said.

"I suppose you think that's a motive for murder." His face turned red.

"I'm not accusing you of anything," I said. "I'm just trying to get to the bottom of things."

I was nervous to ask my next question, but there was one more thing I wanted to find out before I left him.

"I heard a key fob was found in the same alleyway, right after your wife was murdered. It was for a Toyota."

"So? A lot of people drive Toyotas," he said.

"Well, I went to the car dealership, and they gave me the information that you had replaced yours right after the murder. Did you lose your key fob?" I asked. I was making a wild guess, but Thomas had the strangest look on his face, as if he knew he'd been caught.

"All right, we fought that night because she said she was going back to the bakery. Again. And I didn't want her to do that. Enough was enough. She had to let it go."

"And?"

"And we argued in the alleyway and I guess I lost the key fob there. I never would have killed my wife."

"Is that right, Thomas? What about the insurance policy?"

"That has nothing to do with her being murdered. It was just something that I did for security. I made one for myself too. Mallory was the beneficiary on that. She could've easily killed me."

"But she didn't. And you could've gotten that policy for yourself just so that you could say this exact thing."

"I think our conversation here is over. I don't have to tell you anything else. The police haven't arrested me. I had nothing to do with it."

He slammed the door in my face. I turned around to leave. I didn't want him to call the police and have Ash show up. I headed to my car, thinking about what Thomas had said. If he and Mallory had been at breakfast that morning, why would Suzette lie about Mallory stealing her recipe book? Maybe I needed to ask Suzette some more questions.

* * *

I'd finally made it back to the bakery. As I stepped inside, a wave of joy crashed over me. The sweet smell of baked goods filled the air, carrying with it the promise of comfort and satisfaction. The chairs were tucked neatly under the tables, and the last traces of powdered sugar still clung to the countertop like confetti after a parade. The air carried the faint sweetness of butter and vanilla, a reminder of the day's work. Through the front window, the streetlamps cast a soft glow across the empty shop, and for a moment, I stood in the quiet, letting the satisfaction of a full day's labor settle over me. This was my safe haven. Or so I'd thought. Now I wasn't so sure. Not knowing when the killer might show up took away the safe feeling I'd always experienced.

Grandma Ruth stood in the kitchen, her hands on her hips and a disapproving frown etched on her face. "Well, what do you have to say for yourself, Madeline? You disappeared off the face of the earth without so much as a peep!" she exclaimed.

I sheepishly shuffled my feet, trying to muster up an excuse as Grandma Ruth continued her tirade. It felt like I was eight years old again.

"I been waiting' here by the phone, waiting for your call. And what do I get? Not a word from you, not even a holler or a hoot!" Grandma Ruth scolded, her voice rising with each word.

"But Ruth, I texted you . . ." I began meekly.

"No excuses," Grandma Ruth retorted, wagging her finger in my direction. "I ought to make you do fifty push-ups for making me worry."

"Fifty push-ups?" I couldn't help but chuckle at Grandma Ruth's dramatics, despite feeling guilty for causing her to worry. "I can maybe do two if I'm lucky. I promise I'll do better about keeping in touch. Cross my heart and hope to die."

She softened at my sincere apology, her stern expression melting into a warm smile. "Well, all right then, sugar. Just don't let it happen again," she said, her voice gentler now.

I nodded emphatically. "You got it. From now on, you'll be the first person I call, I promise."

Back in the kitchen, I found myself humming a melody as I worked my hands quickly and efficiently, preparing my dough and pastries with care. Baking was like medicine for my soul. It was its own form of therapy; it gave me a sense of purpose and made me feel connected to something bigger. This was my passion, my lifeblood. I was proud of my little bakery, and I could tell it was a source of joy to many. Nothing brought me more pleasure than knowing that what I did brought happiness to so many around me.

I jumped at the sharp rap on the back door. The day's heat still clung to the air as I eased it open. The last streaks of golden light stretched long across the alley. James stood there, his silhouette etched against the fading glow, and a devilish grin tugging at his lips. I tried to process what this meant. I hadn't known James long, and since he'd returned, I had been confused with my feelings. I had walked away from him pretty easily once before, in favor of family and career. But he had come looking for me. Grandma Ruth had warned me away from the temptation of James. Yet here he was, standing at the door, quietly asking me to come outside. The back door—his insistence on using the back entrance was really growing irksome.

I stepped outside, my eyes never leaving his stare.

"I wasn't expecting to see you here right now," I said. "Why don't you use the main entrance like everyone else?"

"I'm not like everyone else. And I wanted to come by and talk to you."

"What about?" I asked.

"I spoke with Thomas and . . ."

"And what?" I pressed.

"I don't know . . . I got a strange vibe from him today."

"Really?" I said. "How so?"

"He said he was leaving town. He quit his job and he's moving away, and I find that highly suspicious considering that his wife was just murdered. It's like he wants—"

"To avoid being caught," I said, finishing the statement for him.

"Exactly," James said. "It just seems odd. Would the police even allow him to leave town right now?"

I would have to ask Ash about that. I knew didn't want me investigating the murder, but if I had relevant information about the case, then I would think he would want to know it. He didn't need to know that I'd gotten the info from James. I had a feeling Ash didn't want me talking to James at all.

My heart beat fast as James and I stood face to face. His gaze burned into mine as he said, "It's always good to see you, *chérie*."

There was something in the way he said it, something in his voice that seemed to cut through the awkwardness, that seemed to spark a flame inside of me. I felt an electric charge in the air, a connection that was palpable.

I couldn't help but smile, caught up in the moment, and all I could do was nod my head. At that moment, a movement to the right caught my attention. Ash had entered the alleyway and was headed our way. He was staring at James. Was he really jealous? I didn't know for sure, but I didn't want to make Ash upset either.

"I guess I should get back to work," I said.

James nodded, a hint of disappointment in his eyes. He took my hand in his, lightly kissing the back of it.

"I'll call you," he said.

"Thanks for the information about Thomas," I said.

As James walked away, I allowed myself one last glance in his direction.

"What was that all about?" Ash asked me as soon as James had disappeared.

I could tell by the tone of his voice that he was not pleased about what had just happened. I sighed heavily as I tried to think of an explanation that would satisfy him without revealing too many details about what I'd learned from James.

"He stopped by to say hi," I said, which was half true.

Ash grumbled something under his breath but didn't press any further for details, which I was grateful for.

We stood in silence for a moment until he finally said, "I worry about you. I don't want you getting hurt."

I nodded solemnly. "I know you don't, and I promise I am keeping an eye out for danger." I really was thankful that Ash had been looking out for me even if it meant risking his own peace of mind. "James gave me some information that I found interesting," I said. I had no choice but to tell him what I knew.

Of course James hadn't been the only source of that information. He just reiterated what I already knew. That Thomas was moving away, but I hadn't known that he'd also quit his job. At least if I told Ash that I had found out this information from James, he wouldn't know that I'd been snooping around trying to solve the murder.

"James says that Thomas, Mallory's husband, quit his job and is moving. And that his house is for sale." I added the last part. Ash didn't need to know that I'd been to the open house.

"I'm aware of all that," Ash said.

"You are?" I asked.

"Is that a surprise to you? I am the lead detective on the case."

"No, it's not a surprise at all," I said. "I just wanted to make sure that you knew."

"You're not trying to find the killer, are you?" he asked, staring right at me.

"What makes you think that?" I said, trying to deflect the question.

"I just want to reiterate that I don't want you to do that. It's a bad idea and it's dangerous."

"Well, does this mean that Ruth is no longer a suspect?" I asked.

"In whose eyes?" Ash asked.

"In your eyes. The only ones that matter," I said.

He stared at me for a long moment. "I've told you before that I don't think she's capable of murder."

"Why don't you tell that to everyone else in town?" I asked. "Because I think the rumors are starting to swirl a little bit too hard."

"I'll find who did this, Madeline, and then everyone will know that you and your grandma had nothing to do with it," he said. "But the pressure is definitely mounting. The longer we go without finding the killer, the harder it's going to be.

The first forty-eight hours are the most crucial. And we're past that."

"Maybe we can work together to solve this," I said.

He shook his head. "Maybe you should just make some croissants, and I'll go find the killer."

"Are you saying I'm not capable?"

"Don't read more into this," he said. "I didn't say that at all."

"But it's what you're thinking, right? That I should stick to the kitchen and let you handle the rest?"

"No, of course not," he said. "Don't put words in my mouth."

I knew I could find the killer. I *would* find the killer. I didn't watch those true crime shows for nothing.

Ash's phone chimed and he checked the screen. "I have to go, but remember what I said?"

"Okay, yeah." I looked away, avoiding his intense gaze.

"Madeline," Ash said.

I nodded. "Yeah, yeah, I'll talk to you soon."

I could feel the weight of his footsteps, heavier than usual, as he walked away from me. I stood frozen in the warm air, struggling to find a way forward, but I felt no closer to a solution. Despair was creeping up within me, like a dark fog slowly consuming my spirit.

A voice came from inside. A familiar voice, one that always made me feel better. I spun around and saw Grandma Ruth as she approached.

"Was that Ash I saw? What did he say?" Grandma Ruth asked.

I shrugged. "No much. Just that he's looking for the killer and I shouldn't."

"It's *our* reputation and freedom on the line, though," she said. "You and I can take this challenge on together. We'll find the murderer."

I hesitated for a moment, still uncertain whether I should keep searching. But the warmth in her voice and the determination in her eyes convinced me.

Without another thought, I nodded. "We have to find out the truth. And time is running out."

Chapter Twenty-Five

My mind raced as I lingered in the bakery long after it had closed for the day, surrounded by the familiar and sweetly comforting smell of baked goods. I still hadn't gotten a call back from the Toyota dealership. I'd actually made the call that I'd lied to Thomas about doing earlier. That was my best lead right now.

Adrenaline surged within me and I shot up out of my seat, snatching my keys and leaving the bakery with haste. I had to get to the car dealership right away and ask some questions. If they wouldn't tell me over the phone, maybe they would in person. A sense of purpose surged through me. I was ready to face whatever consequences awaited me. Desperation clawed at me, demanding answers. I drove quickly to the dealership, which I noted was close to Thomas's house.

I pulled into the parking lot of the dealership and almost leapt from my car. I parked in the giant lot made up of rows upon rows of shiny new cars. The air was hot and heavy with exhaust from the other cars in the place. Inside, the walls were mirrored, so I could see myself reflected on all sides: my brown hair frizzing up all over my head. They probably thought I was some kind of loon who wandered into their place by accident.

The scent of leather seats, rubber tires, and new plastic engulfed me as I headed straight to the service desk and hoped someone would help me. I spotted a lone employee standing at the service desk and rushed over to him. As I hurried through the bustling car dealership, a salesman locked eyes with me and immediately rushed toward me. I was greeted by the overly enthusiastic salesman, whose grin stretched from ear to ear.

"Hello there, ma'am! Welcome to Big Joe's Toyota Emporium, where we make dreams come true on four wheels!" the salesman exclaimed, his voice brimming with excitement.

I offered a polite smile in return, trying to mask my true intentions as I glanced around the showroom. "Thank you. I'm actually just here following up on a call, to inquire about a lost key fob. I believe the previous owner of a certain vehicle may have some information that could be helpful in the investigation of a crime," I explained, keeping my tone neutral.

But the salesman seemed undeterred by my lack of interest in purchasing a car. Instead, he launched into his sales pitch with unwavering enthusiasm. "Ah, a woman on a mission, I like it! Now, let me tell you, we've got the finest selection of vehicles this side of the Sierras. From sleek sedans to rugged SUVs, we've got something for everyone!"

I nodded politely, resisting the urge to roll my eyes at the salesman's relentlessness. "That's great, but I'm really just here to—"

But before I could finish my sentence, he was already leading me toward a row of gleaming cars, extolling the virtues of each model with fervor. "Now, this here beauty is our top-of-the-line model, complete with all the bells and whistles. And just imagine yourself cruisin' down the highway with the wind in your hair . . ."

I sighed inwardly, resigned to the fact that I would have to endure the salesman's pitch before I could get any information. As he continued his spiel, I couldn't help but wonder if I would ever manage to escape the clutches of Big Joe's Toyota Emporium with my sanity intact. When the salesman paused and waited expectantly for my thoughts on the car he was showing me, I took my opportunity.

"Actually," I said, my voice quivering slightly. "Do you have any records of a key fob being replaced for a customer recently? It's part of an official investigation." I opened my wallet and briefly held it up to him, as if I had a badge. I was pretty sure I could get into a lot of trouble for doing it. I would just say I had been showing him my Costco membership card, which was true. It seemed to do the trick, as he finally stopped trying to sell me a car and listened.

"Well," he said, a bit taken aback. "We do have records here, but I'll need to know who the customer is first."

"Thomas," I said without hesitation. "Thomas Gates."

The man seemed to size me up for a moment before nodding and motioning for me to follow him. We made our way to the back office, where he tapped away at a keyboard looking for info. My hands trembled as I waited, my entire body buzzing with excitement.

The man looked over at me. "Yes, it looks as if he did order a replacement fob recently."

He showed me the screen. The date of the order was after the murder. I had to assume Thomas had lost his key fob right before the murder . . . or during it.

"Thank you!" I said as I rushed out of the dealership.

As I drove away, I wasn't sure what to do with the information I had just discovered. I mean, all of this was seemingly leading me to Thomas, but how would I prove that? He had taken out the insurance policy without Mallory's knowledge. Mallory had moved out before her murder. They had had a fight. He'd replaced a key fob right after one had been discovered at the crime scene. What more evidence did the police need?

Chapter Twenty-Six

By the time I got back to the bakery and told Grandma Ruth about the fob, she'd done some investigating of her own. Through town gossip, she'd found out that Mallory had been staying at Natalie's place, in a room she was renting out. According to Grandma Ruth's sources, which aligned with what Thomas himself had said, Mallory had had enough of her husband and decided to leave him. I couldn't say that I blamed her. I mean, I would have left him too if I had discovered he had taken out a life insurance policy on me.

So now I was headed to Natalie's house in the hopes that I would be able to convince her to let me have a look around Mallory's old room. But what would I say to her to get her to agree? Of course I had brought some of my pastries as an incentive. Maybe if she was so grateful that I brought her the sweets she would allow me to take a peek around. I knew she had a sweet tooth. It was worth a shot, so I'd have to give it a try.

I pulled over to the curb in front of Natalie's house, my car's tires screeching against the asphalt as I slammed on the brakes. Her three-story stood tall and forbidding in the older section of town. The Victorian beauty loomed over the other houses like a queen on her throne.

As I approached the porch, the stench of decay hit me like an invisible wall. The flowers in all of the pots were wilted and rotting, adding to the fetid aroma which filled the air. Despite my growing unease, I pounded on the door, every thud echoing like a death knell in my ears. I hadn't expected Natalie to open the door so quickly. She eyed me suspiciously at first and then finally she smiled.

"Hello, Madeline. What brings you here?"

I thrust the box of pastries at her. "I brought these for you."

She eyed the box for a second and then took them. "Why, thank you. For what do I owe this pleasure?"

That was a good question. How would I answer? I couldn't come out immediately and say I wanted to have a look around . . . could I? She stared at me expectantly. I really had no other excuse for being there. I supposes I would just have to play on her sympathy and tell her the truth.

"All right, the truth is I wanted to know if I could have a look around Mallory's room. I'm hoping that her belongings haven't been collected or moved yet. And well, you know I found her in the alleyway behind my bakery. I want to find out who killed her so I can clear my name. And Grandma Ruth's. You can understand that, can't you?"

Natalie stared at me for a long moment and then, to my surprise, she stepped out of the way and gestured for me to come inside. "Just don't tell anybody I did this, okay? Because I think the police probably would frown upon it."

"Mum's the word," I said gratefully. I also didn't want Ash to know about this, so I certainly wouldn't say anything.

As I stepped into the house, a wave of strawberry perfume filled the air, overpowering my senses. The furniture was an eclectic mix of antique pieces that echoed the house's exterior. Every piece seemed to be perfectly placed, as if they had been honed and polished to the peak of perfection.

"It's upstairs to the right. Follow me," Natalie said, motioning.

We climbed the old rickety staircase to the top of the landing and turned to the right.

"It's not locked or anything, but I haven't touched any of her belongings. I would never," she said.

"Oh, I believe you."

She opened the door and let me walk in. "I'll just stand out here in the hallway."

"Thank you," I said.

I hesitantly stepped into the immaculately tidy room, feeling like an intruder in someone else's space. The air in the room hung heavy around me, as if the room had been closed up for years, harboring secrets and dark intentions. I wasn't really sure what I was even looking for. I just hoped there might be some kind of clue.

"The police were already here and looked at everything," Natalie said from the hallway.

"Yeah, I'm sure. But you never know," I said with a shrug.

She grimaced as if she had a little hope that I would find anything that would lead me to the killer. I had the same doubts, but I was trying anything that I could think of at this point. I didn't want to leave any stonc unturned.

I swiveled my head to look around the room. A bed, dresser, and closet filled up most of the space, and a tiny nightstand sat in the corner. The bed was perfectly made with crisp sheets and a bedspread, and everything was neatly put away. I knew Mallory hadn't liked me, but I hoped she would be okay with me invading her former space like this. Maybe things would be different if she'd known I was trying to help her.

First, I checked the closet. I found only clothes hanging in there. What had I expected to find? A skeleton? Next, I walked over and pulled up the bottom of the white bedspread, looking under the bed. There was nothing there, not even a dust bunny. I went over to the dresser and started opening up drawers. More clothing filled the first drawer, but the second one contained a file folder. Of course I pulled it out and looked inside. Recipe cards. I recognized the cards right away. They had the same cherry print at the top like the one I'd found in the dumpster. No way was that a coincidence.

I flipped through the cards and saw the éclair recipe that Mallory had been convinced that I had copied. But this recipe was nothing like my own. When I glanced down at the drawer again I saw a book. When I grabbed it and opened it up, I saw Suzette's name printed on the inside. It was her stolen recipe book! I quickly searched through the rest of the room, but nothing surpassed my discovery of the recipe cards and stolen book. Natalie was patiently waiting for me when I emerged back out into the hallway.

"Thanks for letting me look around," I said nervously. I had hidden the recipe book under my shirt because I didn't think that Natalie would want me to take anything out of the room. But as far as I was concerned, it was Suzette's property and she was getting it back.

"No problem," Natalie said. "I just hope they find the killer soon." She stared at me a long moment, as if trying to decide if I really was the killer or not.

"I do too. I really do," I said. "Well, I should be going."

Natalie walked behind me back down the stairs.

"I hope you enjoy the éclairs," I said, pausing by the front door.

I prayed she didn't notice the book under my shirt. If she realized I'd taken something she'd think I was a thief. And if she thought I was a thief, then she'd surely think I was a killer too.

"I know I will. Thank you so much," Natalie said.

After I said goodbye, I stepped out of the house and hurried down the sidewalk toward my car. I finally felt like I might be a couple steps closer to solving the murder. The humid air clung to my skin as I slid into the driver's seat, the scent of freshly baked bread still lingering on my clothes. I turned the key, and the engine sputtered to life, the weak blast of the AC doing little to cut through the heat.

It had been a long day at the bakery, and all I wanted was to get home, kick off my shoes, and let the ceiling fan do its job. The early evening twilight painted the sky in warm hues. The road shimmered faintly with leftover heat from the sun, and my tires crunched over loose gravel as I turned onto Main Street. The town looked peaceful, with porch lights flickering on and a couple of kids riding bikes down the sidewalk.

As I drove toward the outskirts of town, I glanced in my rearview mirror and noticed a car. Blue, sleek, and trailing me just close enough to make me pay attention.

It wasn't unusual to have someone behind me on this road—it was a shortcut to the next county—but something about the way the car hovered a little too close made the hair on my arms stand up. I eased off the gas, letting the car behind me catch up or, better yet, pass. But it didn't. Instead, it slowed too, maintaining the same uncomfortable distance.

Maybe I was imagining things, I told myself, though my grip tightened on the steering wheel. The warm air from my cracked window blew strands of hair into my face as I turned onto a side road lined with trees. The blue car followed.

Okay, Madeline. Don't freak out. It's just a coincidence.

But my heartbeat picked up as I saw the car inch closer, its presence looming behind me. The setting sun made the road ahead hazy, but I squinted and kept driving, testing the car with another turn. It stuck with me, every move deliberate and unnerving. The humid night wrapped around me like a sticky blanket, and I flicked on my blinker, even though no one else was on the road.

"All right," I muttered, forcing a steadiness into my voice that I didn't feel. "Let's see what you want."

I turned sharply onto a dirt path that led past the old orange grove, the scent of damp earth and summer blooms wafting in through the window. The blue car hesitated, just for a moment, and then followed again, its headlights bouncing over the uneven terrain.

My pulse thundered, my mouth dry despite the thick, moist air. I decided to make a loop and head back into town. I didn't want this car to follow me all the way home. I had to get away from this person.

Chapter Twenty-Seven

I slammed my foot down hard on the accelerator as my car tore through traffic, desperately trying to evade the vehicle hot on my tail. Fear grabbed at my heart like a vice. The sun had suddenly disappeared, giving way to a tumultuous summer storm. The air was alive with electricity as the storm descended. Flashes of lightning lit up the sky in blinding brilliance, while thunder rumbled and roared like a colossal giant marching across the land. The echoes of its steps reverberated in the bone-shaking explosion of sound. The heavens shook in fury as the elements clashed in an explosive display of strength.

Now the streets were slick and the sound of the rain drumming on the car's roof was like a heartbeat in my ears. I caught a glimpse of the blue car in my rearview mirror and saw that it was still there, despite my maneuvering and the turn in the weather. Suddenly, a sharp turn revealed a slim alleyway. I took the chance and spun the wheel, quickly angling my car into the tight space. I watched in the mirror and saw the blue car miss the opening, driving straight past. I took a deep breath and let out a sigh of relief.

But my relief was short-lived. I heard a loud crash behind me and looked in my mirror to see that the other car had reversed and managed to also get into the alley. Terror coursed through me as I realized there was no escape, as I was now blocked from exiting. I frantically bolted from my car, as if abandoning a sinking ship. My adrenaline was pumping as I sprinted down the alleyway. My mind raced for a solution as I frantically scanned the alley for some way to escape.

In the distance, I saw a fire escape and without a moment's hesitation, I dashed toward it. I could hear footsteps behind me. I hadn't even been able to climb the rope in gym class when I was a kid. What made me think I would be able to scamper up this ladder now at my age? I couldn't even get off the sofa without groaning. Blood roared in my ears as I frantically tried to scramble up the ladder to the fire escape.

My fingers slipped on the cold metal rungs and fear coursed through me. A man's voice echoed up the alley, but I couldn't make out the words. With every twist and turn of the ladder, I felt sure I'd fall, never to get away from this nightmare. Suddenly a hand clawed at my dangling ankle. With a final burst of exertion, I pulled myself up, barely escaping the hand grasping at my foot.

I frantically kicked and fought the person off. I heard them stumble backward, giving me the opportunity to run to the opposite side to leap off the fire escape and onto the pavement below. Thank goodness the bottom of the platform almost touched the ground or I would have broken a leg. I felt like Wonder Woman. The adrenaline had given me superpowers. I'd pay for it the next day, though. If I got away through this, I'd have to double up on the Aleve.

Using every ounce of strength left in my body, I sprinted away. I didn't stop running until I reached the safety of my shop. My stomach clenched as I fumbled for the keys to my shop door. I was struggling to find the right one when I heard a deep voice calling my name. I whipped around and saw a dark-haired man mere feet away—the man in the hoodie that I had seen before. I braced myself for impact.

"What do you want?" I demanded, barely able to get the words out.

He eyed me with an intense stare but spoke calmly. He held his hands up. "I'm not here to hurt you. I'm a private investigator."

Was he telling the truth? But he reached into the inner pocket of his shirt and pulled out a business card. With a shaky hand I took it and read:

Paul McMillan. Private investigator.

The words were written in black letters with a phone number underneath.

"What do you want with me?" I asked.

For all I knew this could still all be made up. After all, I'd pretended to be an investigator too. I hadn't made business cards, though. Maybe next time.

"Why were you following me?" I demanded, my voice rising.

The private eye shifted his weight and looked around nervously, as if someone was watching him from the passing cars.

"I'm here about Mallory's murder," he said.

"Who hired you?" I asked, narrowing my eyes.

"The life insurance company," he said, a bead of sweat rolling down his forehead. "And I wanted you to be aware that I've been following you."

"Yeah, I know. You may want to work on your surveillance skills," I said.

He gave me a frown but continued, "The reason I wanted to speak to you is because I've seen a couple other people following you. Not just me."

I peered into the street suspiciously, trying to spot if anyone was potentially watching us. "Who?" I asked, turning back to him.

He shrugged. "I don't know. That's why I'm telling you."

"Isn't that your job to know who they are?"

He shook his head. "I tried to find out, but they gave me the slip. If I do find out, I'll be in touch. I just wanted to warn you."

I nodded. "Thank you. I appreciate you telling me."

And just like that, he was gone. I glanced around one more time. A chill ran up my spine. I hurried into the bakery, thankful to be safe—for now.

Chapter Twenty-Eight

Morning came quickly and I found myself once again elbow deep in pastries. I took a break to take out the trash and when I stepped out the bakery's back door I saw white roses propped against the wall outside. Were the flowers for me? Why were they at the back door? James could've sent them. Or maybe even Ash? But no, he probably wouldn't send me flowers. Why did I feel a bit of disappointment at the thought? I suppose a girl could wish for a sweet gesture, but something was telling me that this wasn't that.

I walked over to the roses. Slipping my fingers beneath the soft petals, I pulled out an envelope that held a card. The note inside was written in elegant French script:

Je parie que tes baisers sont comme des petits macarons, doux et exquis. Tes câlins sont comme des betteraves chaudes, réchauffant mon cœur.

"What have you got there?"

I jumped and spun around. "Ruth. I didn't know you were right behind me."

"Where else would I be, dear?" she asked.

"You could announce yourself. For heaven's sake we found a dead body in this alleyway, so I'm a bit jumpy."

"You don't have to remind me of that. It's lodged forever in my brain." She looked at the flowers. "Oh, roses. From Ash?"

"I don't know," I said with a sigh.

"Oh, no. Is there a card?"

"Yeah." I pulled out the card and handed it to her.

She glanced at it and said, "It's in French? Maybe they're from James."

I shook my head. "The French isn't that good. I think it's from someone pretending to speak French, you know?"

"What does it say?" Grandma Ruth asked.

"'I bet your kisses are like little macarons, sweet and exquisite. Your hugs are like warm beets, warming my heart.'"

"Beets?" Grandma Ruth asked with a frown.

I nodded. "Yeah, beets. I'm pretty sure these are from Frankie, even though I told his mother to have him knock it off."

We headed back into the kitchen. It was time to focus on work and push thoughts of murder from my mind. We had a lot of baking to do.

Later, I was only halfway done with a batch of petit fours when I received a call from James.

"Good morning to you. Did you get the roses I left you?"

"Oh, so those were from you?!" I asked with surprise.

"Yes, they were from me. I guess you were expecting someone else?" he said.

"No," I said nervously laughing. "I just wasn't expecting it at all."

I didn't want to embarrass him by asking about the weird note and the use of the word "beets." Maybe he thought it was poetic. Maybe it was just a typo. It's not as if I spoke French all that well to figure out what romantic word was close to "beets" to misuse.

"Well, I just wanted to make sure you got them. I know that you love white roses," he said.

"Actually . . . I don't. They remind me of a funeral."

"Oh, my mistake," he said. "I must have misunderstood. I'm glad you got them, though. Um, how about that date tonight? We can have a picnic in the park and enjoy the stars. I'll bring the food. All you have to do is show up."

Actually, I don't think tonight works for me," I said.

"Oh," he said with heavy disappointment in his tone. "What about this afternoon? Are you free at four?"

"Sure. I'd like that."

"Perfect. Listen, I have to go, Madeline, but I'll see you soon."

"Thank you again for the flowers," I said. "They *are* beautiful."

I felt like he'd rushed off the call. Had he been upset with this change of plans? Now I felt really bad about telling him that white roses weren't my favorite. Who had told him that they were? I leaned down and smelled one of the roses.

"For heaven's sake," Grandma Ruth said, waving a spatula through the air. "The way you spoke to him just now it's a miracle you ever get a date."

"Thanks a lot, Grandma," I said, swirling some icing on top of a petit four.

"We just have to work with what we've got, I guess," she said.

There were some similarities between James's note with the roses and the earlier notes I'd received in French. It made me wonder. Was *he* the one leaving those notes for me? Had I misunderstood the notes, and they weren't threats at all? Or had I misread James and was he dangerous? It wasn't like I could ask him. He wouldn't come out and admit to it. But maybe I could try to coax it out of him. Maybe on the date we had planned. My romantic date was suddenly morphing into an interrogation. Maybe Grandma Ruth was right about the state of my love life.

Chapter Twenty-Nine

When I arrived at the park, James was waiting for me. He was standing like a statue under the canopy of trees. The park was a lush paradise, the trees standing tall in various shades of green, like sentinels of an ancient kingdom. A small lake sparkled in the sunlight, like a diamond waiting to be discovered. shimmering and inviting. The afternoon felt alive with energy, overflowing with beauty and promise. And maybe a bit of discovery.

James had created a picturesque scene, complete with a red and white checked blanket and a basket full of food. I spotted a loaf of French bread sticking out from the top of the basket. As I stepped toward him, my heart beat faster with excitement. I wondered if my hair was mussed or if there were any wrinkles in my dress that might make me look like a hot mess. I'd rushed home to get ready for the date, taking care to change into my favorite sundress, a vibrant yellow with dainty white flowers. The fabric fluttered gently in the breeze, sending small ripples through the skirt.

"I'm so glad you're here," James said, wrapping his arms around me in a hug.

He looked as handsome as usual. He smelled good too, like old books, cinnamon and pepper. We settled down on the blanket and opened up the basket full of tantalizing treats: sandwiches, small cakes, cookies, and much more.

"Wow, you really went all out for this," I said as I accepted glass of champagne from his hand.

I couldn't help thinking about how he hadn't gotten any of the baked goods from my own bakery but rather from Natalie's. *Focus, Madeline, focus.* We munched away while discussing our future plans for world domination, laughing at each other's jokes and occasionally stealing glances when we thought the other wasn't noticing.

I was trying to focus on James's words. He was telling me about a hiking trip he took years ago to the Swiss Alps. He went into detail about the towering peaks, pristine lakes, and picturesque villages.

"It was like stepping into a postcard. I captured some incredible shots that still transport me back to that moment. But the view wasn't as beautiful as what's in front of me now."

I felt myself blush and was uncertain how to respond. But James kept going.

"I have some news for you. I've gotten along well with the owners of the vineyard and they've offered me a job. Chief sommelier for their tasting room and restaurant. And I'm going to take them up on their offer."

"You've leaving LA—"

"And moving to Solvang," James finished for me.

"Isn't this a bit . . . abrupt? You have a job and a whole life back in the city."

"Is it any different from what you did?" James countered. "As I recall, you made up your mind pretty quickly when you departed."

He had me there.

"Besides, I've seen how you've flourished here. Owning your own place, baking your own recipes . . . you have more freedom. You seem happier, lighter. Apart from the . . . you know, the murder. I'm kind of envious. It seems like there's a lot more freedom in a place like this than at a stuffy restaurant."

At his mention of Mallory's murder, I had a hard time focusing on the rest of what James was saying. I suddenly had an uneasy feeling. I really needed to get a grip on my anxiety. Though I had reason to be nervous after all I'd been through the last few days. I hoped I wouldn't be sick with fear for the rest of my life. I knew I should be happy in this moment. I desperately grasped for something to cling to, a sense of security that seemed just out of my reach. I needed to ask James about the note I'd received with the flowers. I'd be able to tell if he was being honest with me. At least I hoped so. I liked to think my detective skills were that good.

I took a sip of my champagne and then said, "Um, about the note with the roses. Beets?"

He raised an eyebrow. "What do you mean? What about beets?"

I explained what the note had said. "Is my French that bad? Or was that what you meant?" I asked.

He frowned. "But I didn't leave a note with the roses, Madeline."

A chill raced up my spine. Had Frankie added that note? Why would he do such a thing?

"But there was a note," I insisted.

James frowned. "If there was, then it wasn't from me. I bet it was from Ash. That guy hates me. He doesn't want me anywhere near you."

I shook my head. "I just don't think he would do something like that. I think I know who would though," I said.

Just then, out of the corner of my eye, I spotted someone move hurriedly behind one of the nearby trees. I squinted to see if I could spot movement anywhere else. I'd only seen the back of the person, so I couldn't tell if it was Frankie, the private investigator, or someone else entirely.

James's gaze hardened as he asked me, "What's wrong?"

I rubbed my arms as if fighting off a chill even though it was warm outside. "I thought I saw someone watching us." I gestured toward the direction of a giant tree.

James turned to face the direction I had pointed out. "Where? I'll go talk to them." He tensed as if ready to fight whatever danger lurked there.

The park seemed isolated now. The breeze whipped my hair in front of my face as I stared out at the dark line of trees in the distance. I squinted into the shadows, expecting maybe to see a man emerge from behind the trunk of an ancient oak. "He's gone now. It was probably just someone walking in the park," I said but wasn't convinced.

"Let's go," James said, standing up.

As we walked toward the parking lot, the sound of a twig snapping made my breath catch in my throat. I scanned the area for signs of movement, but there were none. Soon enough we had reached the line of trees, but there was nothing there other than a squirrel skittering across the grass.

James stayed closed as we walked, his protectiveness and warmth making me feel safer. "When we get back to our cars, I can follow you home," he said.

As we headed into the parking lot, a different sound caught my attention. It was faint at first, but I soon recognized that it was a car engine. The vehicle was still far away, but I thought I could make out the sight of Ash's car. Why would he be here? Had he followed me? Had he been the one behind the tree? I really didn't think he would do something like that.

James must have sensed my unease. He whispered reassuringly in my ear, "It's okay. I'm here. I won't let anything happen to you."

Though James offered to follow me home, I had other plans. I also needed to call Ash. I was almost sure that it hadn't been him behind the tree. Though I wasn't so sure that hadn't been his car I'd seen just now.

"Thank you, James, for a lovely afternoon, but I just remembered I have somewhere I need to go," I said as I opened my car door.

He looked really confused. "Are you sure? I can come with you."

I kissed his cheek. "No, that won't be necessary. I'll talk to you soon."

With that I climbed behind the steering wheel. When I glanced back, James was still standing by his car, looking forlorn.

Chapter Thirty

I'd managed to find Suzette's address online, and now I drove down her street and pulled up in front of her home. The two-story brick house was charming, but it showed its age. A hedge surrounded the grassy front yard. The street was empty except for a few cars parked along the curb and an old lady walking her dog. There were no cars in the driveway. I wasn't sure what to expect from this trip. I was learning the ins and outs of this investigating stuff the hard way.

I reached into the backseat and pulled out Suzette's recipe book, its cover soft and warm from the sunshine. As I walked up the cracked stone path, the quiet hum of cicadas filled the still air. I knocked on the front door—once, then twice—listening for footsteps, a voice, anything. Nothing.

I pressed the doorbell. The chime echoed faintly inside, but no movement followed. She wasn't home. The porch air sat heavy and undisturbed. Curiosity tugged at me. I stepped off the porch and moved toward the front window, shielding my eyes with my hands as I leaned in. The glass was warm against my forehead. Inside, everything looked tidy—too tidy, like no one had lived in it for days. However, on the end table near the window, a cluttered stack of papers caught my eye. They looked fresh, like someone had just dropped them there in a hurry. Something about them made my stomach stir.

Then I noticed something about them. On top was a recipe card.

It looked just like the ones that Mallory had in her possession. It had a distinctive design, with a little cherry print on top. I wondered if Mallory had stolen Suzette's recipe cards along with the book that I was hoping to now return to her. But it seemed I'd have to come back and try again another time, so I reluctantly departed.

A little while later, as I pulled up to the bakery, my phone buzzed with a call from James.

"How are you?" I asked.

"Not great, to be honest," he replied, his voice heavy with concern.

"What's wrong?"

"Well, I received this very strange note."

"A note?" I asked as I got out of my car.

As soon as I said it out loud it brought back all kinds of feelings about the notes that I had suspected him of leaving me. Was James trying to cause a distraction by pretending he'd also received a note? I had no idea where all these notes were coming from, but it was really beyond weird.

"Yeah, the note said for me to leave you alone. That I shouldn't ever contact you again. Who would do something like that?" he asked.

Immediately Frankie came to mind. Who else would tell James to leave me alone? Ash? Surely he wouldn't do something like that? It seemed like something that an immature teenager would do. Or maybe the P. I. had mistakenly assumed James was stalking me?

"Of course I'm not going to stop talking to you," James reassured me.

"I'll find out who sent the note to you," I said as I grabbed my bag and Suzette's recipe book from my car.

"Not if I find out first," he said with determination. "I'll call you soon."

After I ended the call with James, I walked toward the bakery. Someone called out to me, and I spun around to see Ash approaching. Now I could ask him about the note that James had received. Another uniformed police officer walked with him. The other officer narrowed his eyes and stared at me.

As soon as Ash walked up to me, he fixated on the object in my hand. "What is that?" He'd spotted Suzette's recipe book. "Is that Suzette's recipe book that she said was stolen? Why do you have it?" he demanded.

How would I explain this? My heart raced as I tried to find the right words to explain why I had Suzette's stolen property in my possession. Suspicion colored the officer's face, but I couldn't read Ash's expression. Did he think that I really had been stealing recipes? Not just from Mallory but Suzette too? Did he think I had killed Mallory so I could pin the theft on her?

I replied softly. "Yes, it's Suzette's recipe book that she said was stolen."

Ash's brows furrowed in confusion. He took the book from me and flipped through it.

"How did you get it?" Ash asked.

I hesitated before answering, trying to figure out how to explain what had happened without telling him the whole truth.

"Did you take this from Mallory?" Ash asked.

My breath caught in my throat. The words stung more than they should have—especially coming from Ash. My pulse quickened, not just from the accusation, but from the way his eyes held mine, searching for something.

"No! Of course not! I can't believe you would think something like that."

"I don't want to think that, Madeline, but I have to get a good explanation from you about this."

"I really can't talk about this anymore," I said.

Now I was hurt and angry. I turned and walked away from Ash. He said nothing else and when I finally looked back, he and the officer were already gone.

Chapter Thirty-One

The sun shone brightly in the blue summer sky and I was thankful for the warmth after my cold encounter with Ash. As I walked the rest of the way to the bakery, I glanced over and saw Frankie coming out of the nearby florist. He was carrying a bouquet of white roses. I gritted my teeth, stepped off the curb and onto the street to cross over to the bakery. I looked over just in time to see a car barreling toward me. I felt a sudden tremor and heard the loud roar of an engine. The screeching tires threw off a fine spray of grime and muck. I froze for an instant before throwing myself backward onto the pavement, tumbling onto the sidewalk, pulse hammering, barely missing being struck by a millisecond.

The cracks in the pavement scraped my skin. A man rushed over and helped me to my feet.

"Are you all right, miss?" His voice was laced with worry. "If I didn't know any better, I'd swear that car was *trying* to hit you!"

Taking deep breaths to regain my composure, I brushed away the stray strands of hair from my eyes and simply nodded. The car drove off without stopping, its driver oblivious to the near-fatal incident, leaving me shaken in its wake.

"That car almost hit me," I said, as I realized Thomas's car was the one driving off in the distance. He had tried to run me down with his car.

"Are you sure you're okay?" the man asked again.

I nodded. "Yes, I'll be fine."

"If you're sure . . ." the man said reluctantly.

"Thank you for your help," I said, trying to sound reassuring. "I really appreciate it."

The man slowly made his way back down the sidewalk, glancing over once as if to make sure I was still standing. I watched him depart, lost in my own thoughts. I needed to prove that Thomas had just tried to kill me. Would he come back and finish what he'd started?

Grandma Ruth came running out of the bakery and over to me. She must have seen the whole thing from the bakery window.

"Are you okay, Madeline?"

I nodded, though my throat was tight and my heart felt like it was going to burst from my chest. I let out a deep breath and told her that Thomas had been the driver.

"We need to get that guy," she said with a pump of her fist.

"He's clearly trying to stop me from investigating further."

Grandma Ruth nodded, her face determined. She quickly pulled out her phone from her pocket.

"What are you doing?" I asked.

"I'm going to call Ash."

"I don't want you to do that," I said, touching her arm.

She studied my face for a moment, "Well, then what are we going to do? We can't just let Thomas get away with that."

"I'll think of something," I said as I brushed dirt off my clothes.

"Let's go!" Grandma Ruth commanded, her voice sharp and urgent.

With undeniable power, she marched down the sidewalk, and I followed in her wake. From the set of her jaw, whatever she had planned, she wasn't backing down. This must be what she had looked like to the opposing team from across the football field during the final quarter of a game.

"What are we doing?" I asked, as I rushed along beside her.

"We're going to find Thomas! Now!" she shouted back, fire in her eyes and determination on her face.

"Well, I'm driving, then," I said, a little nervously as we reached my car.

Grandma Ruth nodded briskly without a word and climbed into the passenger seat of my car. "Let's go," she said, pointing straight ahead.

Grandma Ruth sat in silence as I drove, her hands clenched together so tightly that her knuckles had turned white. I kept stealing glances at her, wondering what thoughts filled her mind and what emotions swirled inside her.

When we reached the turnoff for the main road, I felt a wave of apprehension wash over me. I had no idea what Thomas would do next, but I knew that whatever it was, it was going to take all my courage to face him.

Driving through town, I was determined to find Thomas. I frantically scanned every car that we passed. As we drove on, the atmosphere of Solvang surrounded us—its colorful buildings, quaint cafes, and independent businesses. Children laughed in the park, couples held hands, and visitors shared laughter, but I knew now of the darkness that lurked in the shadows of this small town.

I finally spotted the familiar Toyota parked outside the local diner. I gasped and slammed my foot on the brake.

"That's his car!" I shouted, pointing at the vehicle

"I knew he wouldn't get far," Grandma Ruth said calmly beside me.

My body hummed with anticipation as I hastily parked nearby and turned off the engine. "Are you ready for this?" I asked nervously as I pulled my key from the ignition.

"More than ready," she replied tersely.

The smell of sizzling grease and meat permeated the air inside the diner, assaulting our senses. I searched the room, my eyes darting from one patron to another until they landed on Thomas, who sat alone at a corner table, a cap pulled low over his brow and sunglasses hiding his eyes.

Grandma Ruth nudged me sharply in the ribs. "There he is," she whispered through gritted teeth. "Does he think he's fooling anyone with those sunglasses?"

With anxiety coursing through me, we approached him, determined to confront the monster responsible for almost running me over.

I stepped forward and exclaimed, "Thomas!"

Grandma Ruth pushed in closer to the table, her body forming an impenetrable barrier between him and the exit. Thomas looked at us both from behind his sunglasses before settling his gaze on me.

"You almost hit me today. I want to know why," I demanded.

His mouth twisted into a sneer as he said, "I don't know what you're talking about."

"Don't play dumb with us," Grandma Ruth snapped.

"Why are you following me?" he said. "This is harassment!"

"That's rich coming from you!" Grandma Ruth scoffed.

"I'm not following you," I said, my own voice laced with anger. "I know it was you. You almost hit me with your car just now and I think you did it on purpose, which leads me to also believe that you killed your wife. Why else would you want me out of the way?"

"If you don't get away from my table, then I'm going to call the police and tell them that Mallory's killer is right here," he said. He tried to rise from the table, his chair screeching against the floor, but Grandma Ruth had blocked him in like a concrete wall.

"No, you're not," I snapped.

Thomas's voice was like a whip as he bellowed, "Get away from my table, murderer!"

Of course everyone in the diner was mesmerized by our exchange. All chatter had ceased and every head was turned in our direction. The hostess stood by her station, her hand hovering above the phone. She could call the police at any second. This could end badly for me if I didn't keep a cool head. As far as I was concerned, all evidence pointed to Thomas as being the killer, but this scenario wasn't good for any of us, regardless. Confronting him about this any further would do no good in this moment. He wasn't going to admit to anything. I just had to find a way to prove it. Maybe there would be some sort of surveillance video from one of the businesses on the street around town that had captured his vehicular attack.

"Fine," I said. "But I will prove that you did this. And that it was you who killed Mallory."

Grandma Ruth slammed her fist on the table, silverware jumping with the impact. "It's not the last you'll hear of this," she declared, her voice slicing through the hum of the diner like a hot knife through cherry pie.

A hush fell over the room. A fork froze midair, someone's coffee paused just inches from their lips. A waitress standing by the pie case blinked twice, unsure whether to laugh or duck for cover.

Then, without another word, Grandma Ruth and I turned on our heels and stomped out, the bell above the door jingling like it was afraid not to. Behind us, whispers bloomed like wildfire.

"Did she just—?"

"Darn right she did."

"Ruth has always been tough as nails."

By the time we hit the sidewalk, I swear I heard someone clap.

* * *

"Can you believe him?" I said as we marched along the sidewalk toward my car.

"I believe it and I also believe he killed his wife. Why else would he try to kill you? Because you're trying to find out who did it, so he has to put a stop to you. This is too scary, Madeline. We need to go to the police. Ash needs to know."

"I'm handling it," I said as slipped back into my car. "Don't worry."

"How can I not worry? You're always getting into some kind of dangerous situation." She let out an exasperated sigh as I started the engine.

"I think Thomas also sent that note to James," I said.

"What note?" Grandma Ruth asked, so I filled her in on what James had told me.

"We need to see the note James received," Grandma Ruth replied when I was done.

"We should go ask him for it right now," I said, stopping at a red light.

But as we sat at the light, I spotted an all-too-familiar car. Thomas was right behind us.

Chapter Thirty-Two

I glanced up through my rear window and saw Thomas's car directly behind us.

"Um," I said, panicked. "Thomas is following us! Again! We have to lose him!"

She nodded and told me to go faster as she looked nervously back over her shoulder. The light turned green and I punched the gas hard. The car surged forward as if it was alive, racing through the streets and flying past buildings. Thomas was gaining ground fast, and my heart pounded as the adrenaline started to pump through my veins. I had no idea if we were going to escape.

My hands gripped the wheel tightly as I drove the car around a curve and I stepped on the gas even harder. We took the corner with a screech of tires, and I heard Thomas's car following close behind. We roared past Marcus in his horse-drawn carriage as he guided some tourists through the downtown. I saw his passengers' startled faces as we whizzed past. Then, just as suddenly as the chase had begun, the street ahead cleared up, the cars suddenly parted. I pressed down hard on the accelerator and we flew forward, leaving Thomas in our dust.

Grandma Ruth and I both let out a sigh of relief.

"Good job!" Grandma Ruth said. "We had made it. Those were some impressive driving skills."

"It was a life-or-death situation," I said breathlessly.

Minutes later we came to a screeching halt along the curb, the engine ticking as we parked. James had texted me the address earlier. "This has been a crazy day," I said.

"Well, I hope it's about to get better," Grandma Ruth said.

As we headed for the sidewalk, I caught movement out of the corner of my eye. Thomas had pulled up behind my parked car.

"Grandma Ruth, it's him!" I shouted.

"My God! What will it take to get away from this man?! Run!" she said as she grabbed my hand. "We have to get away from here."

Without looking back, Grandma Ruth and I sprinted away from the scene. Gravel crunched under our shoes, adrenaline pushed us forward, and to my shock, Grandma kept pace like she was twenty years younger. Her hair came loose from its clip, silver strands flying behind her like a cape.

"Still got it," she muttered between breaths, not even winded.

We ran until my lungs burned and my legs turned to jelly. I was ready to collapse, but Grandma just kept going. She was determined, wild-eyed, and grinning like she hadn't had this much fun in decades.

Panting with exhaustion, we stumbled toward the bakery. We soon lunged through the door, locking it behind us, and collapsed into a pair of chairs with a loud groan, our limbs heavy and our breaths ragged. Still breathing heavily, I peered out the window for any sign that Thomas might still be nearby, but there was nothing. Slowly but surely, my breathing returned to normal and my terror began to fade.

"Are you going to call Ash *now*?" Grandma Ruth asked with frustration in her voice.

I sighed. "Yes, I will call him."

As I started to dial Ash's number, my phone rang. *He* was calling *me*.

"It's Ash," I said.

"Answer now!" Grandma Ruth said, waving her hand frantically.

"Where are you?" Ash asked when I answered.

"I'm at the bakery. We ran here because Thomas showed up. He tried to run me over earlier."

"I'm looking for him now," Ash said.

"He was over at James's house," I said and gave him the address.

"I just passed there not long ago and he wasn't there."

As I began to answer Ash, I happened to look out the window and sure enough spotted Thomas on the sidewalk across the street. I knew he was searching for me.

"That's because he's here! Now!" I said.

"Stay put," Ash said. "I'm on my way."

I hustled Grandma Ruth away from the front window and into the kitchen. We stayed in the back, out of sight for what felt like hours but was really only a few minutes. If Thomas was still lurking out front, we were too scared to check. Ash arrived in minutes, as promised. We could hear him shouting orders outside. I poked my head above the bakery counter and through the window could see Ash pointing his gun at Thomas. Thomas threw his hands up in the air, looking as terrified as I also felt.

Grandma Ruth and I quickly stepped outside, watching as Ash cuffed Thomas. Others had started to gather on the sidewalk as well to watch the unfolding scene.

"I'm innocent! She's lying!" Thomas declared

My throat went dry. I had no idea what to say now. I knew I had to stay calm and find out the full truth before things spiraled out of control.

"What will happen now?" I asked.

Ash looked at me as he guided Thomas toward his police car. "He's being arrested for his wife's murder. And for your attempted murder."

"Oh, thank goodness. Now maybe we're safe," Grandma Ruth said. "It's finally over."

But I wasn't so sure.

Chapter Thirty-Three

The next day things had seemingly settled down in town. Grandma Ruth was relieved that someone had finally been arrested for Mallory's murder—someone other than her. But I still wasn't convinced about the arrest. I just had an uneasy feeling because I couldn't understand how Suzette's recipe book had ended up in Mallory's possession. Luckily Suzette had just walked into the bakery. I was going to use this opportunity to ask her more questions.

Suzette greeted me as she walked up to the counter. "Good morning, Madeline. I'm so glad that everything has worked out. It seems like your bakery is doing well now." She glanced around at the small cluster of customers but had a funny look on her face when she said it.

"Good morning, Suzette. Good to see you again."

"Can I get a couple of those éclairs?"

"Sure thing," I said. "Which ones?"

Suzette studied the trays inside the bakery case before asking for three classic and three coffee-flavored. After I started preparing her order, I tried to sound casual as I said, "So I still don't understand how Mallory got her hands on your recipe book. Are you convinced it was her who stole it?" I asked.

Suzette tucked a strand of hair behind her ear before answering. "Well, I didn't have my glasses on when it happened or anything. I tend to misplace them."

"Hm." I didn't want to say much, just let her do the talking.

"So I suppose it *could* have been someone else. But I was just so sure it was Mallory."

"Is there anything about the person you can tell me that might help us figure it out?"

"Well, I do remember the person was dressed in jeans and a white T-shirt." Suzette continued, "But I really think it was Mallory because it just seems like something she would have done."

But why would Mallory even want Suzette's recipe book? Unless she really thought that Suzette had stolen her own recipes.? It didn't make any sense. It wasn't like the recipes were valuable.

"Yeah, I guess so" was all I said.

"Well, thanks again for the éclairs," Suzette said after I handed over the box tied with string.

"You're welcome . . . and, oh, by the way, Suzette, those recipe cards that you have. Where did you buy those? The ones with the cherries on the top."

She stared at me for a moment. "Oh I don't remember. A shop here in town, I guess."

"Not many places to buy recipe cards in town," I said.

She eyed me suspiciously. "How did you even know about those cards?"

"I saw them when I stopped by your place earlier. I knocked on the door, but you weren't home. Then I looked in the window because I thought I heard a noise, and I just happened to see some on the table."

She stared at me for a moment longer. "Yeah, well, nice talking to you, Madeline."

With that, she turned and left the bakery. But I had the distinct impression that she had not enjoyed our conversation.

Chapter Thirty-Four

As the sun began to dip lower in the sky, I flipped over the "closed" sign on the bakery door. Grandma Ruth had left earlier to attend to some things at her place. I had been turning over the most recent events in my mind, trying to uncover what had been nagging at me since Thomas's arrest. As I reached my car, I only hesitated for a moment before I made up my mind. I then drove with fierce urgency to Frankie's house. I parked hastily along the curb and raced up to the front door. Frankie's mother answered the door right away. Before I even had a chance to knock. The air between us crackled with tension.

"You again," Mrs. Castille said with disdain.

"I still have some unanswered questions about your son. Is Frankie home?" I asked.

She shook her head and replied with a stern "No, he's not here. And I don't want you to talk to him anyway."

"Well, then, perfect. I can talk to you," I said, pressing my advantage. "You know you can get into trouble with the police for lying?"

Frankie's mother scoffed at the accusation. "Are you accusing my son of something? He's a good boy. He's never done anything wrong."

"I'm not so sure about that. I have an eyewitness who saw your son stealing a recipe book from Mallory's car." I was once again relying on my tactic of making a bold lie and hoping to be led to the truth. It had worked in the recent past and I was hoping it might work again now.

Frankie's mother laughed at me in disbelief. "A recipe book? That child has never wanted to cook. Why would he want recipes?"

"Well, that's what I want to find out," I snarled back.

"Look, I was at work the night that Mallory was murdered. I mean, I heard people talking about it and that they *saw* her husband do it."

"That's a lie!"

Her expression changed in an instant. Her face contorted into a mask of fury and desperation. "Okay, fine, but I . . . I don't want you trying to get Frankie in trouble, because I know he would never do anything to hurt anyone."

"Clearly you have your suspicions or you wouldn't be lying for him now."

"A mother will do a lot for her child," she said.

"Including cover up a murder?" I asked incredulously.

"If need be," she said. "And I think we're done talking now."

She slammed the door in my face. We were clearly done talking, but now I had even more questions. And I was highly suspicious of Frankie. But where would I find him? Did I even want to find him? At the least, I knew I needed to tell Ash about all of this. I hopped back into my car so that I could head home. Before pulling out onto the street, I sent Ash a text message letting him know that I needed to talk to him as soon as possible.

Chapter Thirty-Five

When I got back home, I spotted something on my front porch waiting for me. It was another vase full of white roses. I hurried up the front steps, looking around to see if anyone was nearby. But the street was deserted. I noticed a card sticking up from the middle of the bouquet, so I pulled it out right away. Were these more flowers from James or from Frankie? I just had a feeling that something wasn't right with Frankie.

I decided to send Ash another text. Maybe he would brush this all off as nothing since Thomas had already been arrested. But I still felt unsafe. I felt as if someone was watching me even at this very moment. I hurriedly typed out a text message.

I think something is wrong. Could you come by here? I'm at home. I just have this strange feeling that someone is watching me. Do you know anything about Frankie Castille?

I hit send on the text message and hoped that Ash answered soon. Better yet, I hoped that he came over right away. The sound of footsteps caught my attention and I spun around to see Frankie walking up the path toward me. I considered trying to bolt to a nearby house, but he was mere seconds away. And I felt my fear become overtaken by righteous anger. So instead I turned on the recorder on my phone just in case I needed evidence of whatever was about to happen.

"What are you doing here?" I asked angrily.

"I saw you came to my house again today." He shook his head with a smile. "I knew you'd come around eventually. That if I kept chasing you, you'd finally see that my love is real and you would understand that you have feelings for me too. You always have."

"No, that's not the case at all," I said. "I've told you repeatedly that I want you to leave me alone. Why can't you understand that?"

"It's not the truth," he said, shaking his head.

"What's not to understand? I am *not interested.* Look Frankie, I could have been your friend if you would have just backed off and been normal. But this is not normal. None of this has been normal. So I can't have anything to do with you. I want you to stay away from me. I want you stay away from my house. I want you to stay away from the bakery too. Do you understand me?"

The anger inside me boiled over like a volcano, spewing out hot, molten fury that scorched the air around us. My voice rose to deafening levels as I yelled at him, my face contorted with raw emotion. But he just wouldn't listen, wouldn't back down. The rage inside me intensified until it felt like my whole body was on fire.

"But what about everything I've done for you?" he said.

"What do you mean everything that you've done for me? Stalked me? Freaked me out with threatening notes?"

His face contorted with rage, his eyes narrowing to slits as he clenched his fists so tightly that the knuckles blanched white. "I gave you flowers. I wrote you notes. *Love* notes! I got James and Thomas to leave you alone. I told them to stay away from the bakery. I even took the recipe book from Suzette's car and put it in Mallory's room in order to frame her. I wanted everyone to see that Mallory was the real cheater, not you, and that she couldn't continue to be mean to you. She needed to leave you and your bakery alone. I just want you to be successful. Then we can get married and run away together. We can have a happy life."

I had no idea how serious this situation had become. Frankie's infatuation had gone way beyond anything normal. This was no schoolboy crush; this a dangerous obsession. Had he killed Mallory? For *me*? What was I going to do now? I figured I should stall. I would just have to go along with it, and hope that Ash showed up soon because I felt trapped. I couldn't get away from Frankie. He would run after me if I tried to flee. I had to try to talk to him calmly.

I tried to soften my expression and my tone. I nearly choked on the words, but I managed to say, "Thank you, Frankie, for everything that you've done. I really do appreciate that you care so much for me and want me to be successful. Did you . . . did you kill Mallory for me?"

He crossed his arms and frowned at me. Everything pointed to Frankie. He'd all but admitted it to me. Now I just needed him to actually say the words. I would record it and then this case would truly be solved. So . . . I went on.

"I mean, it would be incredible if you'd done something like that for me, but . . . it was Thomas, wasn't it? I found all kinds of clues that indicate he killed his wife, so I'm assuming he did it and not you. I mean, at least he got rid of her, and I don't have to worry about her anymore, right?" I said with a laugh. "I should thank him."

Even pretending like those were my feelings was making my stomach turn. I felt disgusted at saying such things, but this was life or death and I had to play along with this sick game.

Frankie staggered back, shocked. "What? What do you mean *thank* Thomas? He didn't do that for you. *I* did that for you. *I* killed Mallory. How could you do this to me? How could you betray me like that? After all the love I gave to you. I gave you everything."

His face twisted with unbridled rage, and I was certain that he was about to do the same thing to me as he did to Mallory. My only chance of survival was to get inside my house. But he blocked my way, slowly advancing toward me. I took steps backward, but it felt like walking on quicksand. Each step was harder than the last, until I found myself backed up against the porch steps. Frankie loomed over me, his eyes wild with fury.

Chapter Thirty-Six

Frankie reached behind him with a calm that made my stomach drop. When his hand came back around, it held a gun, gleaming and cold, aimed straight at me.

"Frankie, what are you doing? I thought you loved me?! Look, we can talk about this," I said, pleading with him for my life. "Don't do this. I mean, there will be other women better than me."

"You're right about that," he said bitterly.

"You'll end up in jail if you kill me, and then you'll never meet anyone or be happy. Why would you want to do that?"

"I'm not going to jail," he said. "No one is going to know it was me."

"How's that possible?" I asked. "Thomas is already in jail. Who could you frame for this?"

"I'll just find someone else to blame. Just like I did with Mallory. It worked out. Did you find Thomas's key fob that I stole and planted in the alley? Though it would have been even easier if you hadn't been snooping around—which I tried to stop you from doing, by the way. But you wouldn't listen because you're so stupid. I don't know why I ever liked you in the first place."

There had to be something I could do to get out of this. I knew at any moment Frankie could pull the trigger. *Think, Madeline, think.* Fear surged through me as our eyes locked in an intense, deadly battle of wills. I could see the rage sparking in Frankie's gaze. His twisted love had turned to hate so quickly. He seemed to sense the fear that coursed through me. The seconds stretched out like a wire about to snap.

With one swift movement I snatched the crystal vase filled with delicate roses from atop the step beside me. Giving it a powerful swing, I shattered the vase over Frankie's head. He howled and crumpled beneath its impact. The gun fell, clattering across the walkway. I ran after the gun before Frankie even hit the ground. I awkwardly grabbed the gun up, pointing it at him. I'd never held a gun before and had no idea if I was handling it correctly. But there was no time to think in the moment, only react. I was fighting for my life.

Frankie lay on the walkway, not moving a muscle. His eyes were shut.

"Don't move," I said, my voice hard despite my trembling hands.

As far as I could tell he was out cold, but just in case he heard me I had to warn him. I had no idea what I was going to do next, but I knew I had to act fast or else this would end badly.

"Don't move," I repeated. "Or I'll shoot."

"Madeline, are you all right?" yelled a familiar voice from down the street. Ash came running toward me at last, and I lowered the gun as he approached, holding it out for him to take.

"Are you okay?" Ash asked again, and that was all it took to break the calm, I-can-handle-it aura I'd built around myself: I burst into tears.

"He tried to kill me," I stuttered, pointing to Frankie. "I've got it all on my phone. He killed Mallory."

Grandma Ruth came hastily running up close behind Ash. "What's going on? What's going on?" she repeated frantically.

"Ruth, stay back," Ash ordered sternly.

Grandma Ruth stared in horror as she took in the chaotic scene and realization sank in of just how much danger I'd been in.

"Don't lose that recording, Madeline," Ash said, and I texted the file to him, scared I might somehow delete it or lose it by accident. Ash grabbed Frankie with an iron fist, yanking his torso off the ground to handcuff him.

Frankie stirred, groaning softly in response as he blinked awake. With one swift move, Ash had him upright.

Frankie stirred, a low groan slipping out as his eyelids fluttered. Ash crouched beside him, one hand firm on his shoulder to steady him.

"Easy," Ash muttered, his voice edged with impatience.

The wail of a siren cut through the night, and within moments the EMTs jogged up the sidewalk, gear in hand. They dropped to their knees beside Frankie, shining a light in his eyes, checking his pulse, asking questions he answered.

Ash hovered, jaw tight, and arms crossed, waiting. He didn't like giving up control, but he held back while they wrapped gauze around Frankie's head and declared him stable enough to move.

The instant they stepped aside, Ash swooped in. With a fistful of Frankie's collar, he hauled him upright in one brutal motion.

"All right, Frankie," Ash said under his breath, his tone like steel. "Let's go."

He marched him down the path toward the cruiser, the EMTs watching warily as Ash muscled his prisoner along.

He kept a firm grip on Frankie's arm, just in case he decided to make a break for it. Ash opened the back door of the cruiser and pushed Frankie inside, making sure the handcuffs were securely fastened as he began to read him his rights.

"You could have just loved me back and it would have saved all of this from happening," Frankie said, leaning around past Ash to talk to me, ignoring *you have the right to remain silent*.

Did he really expect me to say something back to him? My throat was dry and my mouth was numb. I had nothing left to say, nothing that would change any of this. Frankie glared at me one last time, his eyes burning with fury. I felt the power radiating from him, and I had to remind myself that he was powerless now. I was safe, at last.

"Well, I've heard of having a crush before, but nothing like that. That boy has lost his mind," Grandma Ruth said.

"You're telling me," I said, releasing a deep breath. "Thank goodness it's all over now."

* * *

As I stood in my bakery the next morning with Grandma Ruth, Pepper's presence was comforting as he wove around my legs. I couldn't help but feel a sense of contentment wash over me. The weight of the recent investigation, the unraveling of the mystery, and the resolution of Mallory's murder had lifted from my shoulders, leaving behind a profound sense of relief and accomplishment. Grandma Ruth had tried to talk me into taking a day off and keeping the bakery closed, but I was craving a return to normalcy.

As if on cue, the brass bell above the bakery door rang out. I looked up to see Ash standing in the doorway, a warm smile lighting up his face. With a soft chuckle, he stepped into the room, his eyes meeting mine with an unspoken understanding.

"Hey there," Ash said, his voice soft and gentle. "I just wanted to stop by and see if you were all right."

"I'm okay," I said. "I think I'll be a little on edge for a while, but I'm all right."

Grandma Ruth beamed proudly at me, her eyes twinkling with affection. "That's my girl," she said, reaching out to give my hand a reassuring squeeze. "You've always had quite the knack for baking . . . and now for solving mysteries too, Madeline."

"Well, not *every* mystery," I said. "There are still some things that are bothering me."

"Like what?" Grandma Ruth protested. "We know now that Frankie killed Mallory."

"Yes, but Thomas also nearly killed *me*. Was that insurance policy he not-so-secretly took out on Mallory just a coincidence? Or was he planning on doing her harm all along and Frankie just beat him to it?"

"Maybe I can clear up at least some of this," Ash volunteered. "Having thoroughly interrogated both of them now, we have a better sense of things. Thomas did come after you—for which he'll be prosecuted to the full extent of the law. But I don't think he ever planned to murder Mallory. He was an unfaithful husband, and a greedy one at that. He was having an affair with Allison Gibbs and wanted his and

Mallory's life insurance sorted out before he left Mallory so it could be folded into their eventual divorce settlement. But Mallory's death delayed his plans to pick up and leave town and the stress of her death and the investigation clearly made him—"

"Cuckoo! Nuts! Crazy as a loon!" Grandma Ruth interrupted. "I could go on—"

"That's okay," I jumped in. "We all get the picture. So who was he meeting at the warehouse that day I followed him? I know it was a woman."

"That would be Allison, his—"

"Mistress," Grandma Ruth interrupted again.

"I guess it's where they would go sometimes to, um . . . link up," Ash said sheepishly. "Distasteful, but not illegal. And the notes were just meant to scare you off."

"Between him and Frankie, a lot of men have been writing me threatening notes lately," I said drily.

"And we now know that it was Frankie who sent you out to the windmill," Ash continued. "All part of his obsession with you and watching you from afar."

"I should have guessed it was Frankie that had me go to the windmill, since that's a spot frequented by teens," I said, frustrated by my rush of hindsight. "It's still so creepy that Frankie's obsessive behavior led to an innocent woman being killed. Because of me."

"You can't think of it that way," Grandma Ruth soothed. "Mallory was simply in the wrong place at the wrong time. So were you."

"All I know is that after the last few days, between Frankie, Thomas, and that private investigator, I've had enough of being chased and followed for a lifetime," I said.

"I admit that I'm a little tuckered out from chasing after them myself," said Ash with a laugh.

"Where'd Frankie get a gun, anyway?" I asked. "Isn't he a little young?"

"It was his mother's," Ash said. "She'll probably face some charges for not storing it securely."

Some part of me was a little glad she'd get in trouble, given how dismissive she'd been of my concerns about her son.

The bell above the door pealed again, and this time James walked in. Grandma Ruth rolled her eyes at the sight of him, and Ash's posture stiffened. But I, at least, was happy to see another familiar face. James came rushing toward me.

"Madeline!" he said breathlessly. "I read in this morning's paper what happened. Are you all right?"

"Good timing, showing up *after* the crazed killer has been arrested," Grandma Ruth said under her breath.

"*Pardon*?" James asked, confused. "What did I miss?"

"Oh, not much," Grandma Ruth said with another roll of her eyes.

"I'll explain everything eventually, James," I said. "Once I feel up to it."

"I guess you'll be making your way back to LA soon?" asked Ash.

"Didn't Madeline tell you? I've decided to stay. I have a job now at the winery. So I can come here every morning for breakfast on my way to work!" James declared excitedly.

Ash said nothing but simply glanced my way, one brow raised. I turned away, unable to meet his eyes. My love life had suddenly gone from nonexistent to very complicated in the span of just a few days. Luckily Grandma Ruth cut through the awkward moment.

"Let's celebrate all this craziness being behind us," she stated. "How does coffee and spandauers sound?"

"Span-dauer"? James asked confusedly.

"I think I'd prefer an éclair," Ash said with a smile directed just at me.

With a soft purr, Pepper nuzzled against my leg. I bent down and scooped him up in my arms. Surrounded by the warmth and love of my grandma, friends, and furry companion, I couldn't help but feel grateful for the bonds that held us together. In that moment, I knew that I was exactly where I belonged. Ready to face whatever challenges lay ahead. For in the embrace of love and friendship, I had found the greatest treasure of all—a sense of hope and a home where my heart truly belonged.

"But please," Ash urged me, "no more investigating murders!"

Acknowledgments

My heartfelt thanks to everyone at Crooked Lane Books for your dedication, guidance, and belief in this story. And to my agent, Jill Marsal, thank you for your support and insight. I am endlessly grateful.